AD A BSUR DUM.

A Novel

To Tristan Tzara,
Salvador Dalí
Neil Gaiman

and

To Mrs. Johnson(s)
Mr. Vaspol

The Pipe

The pipeline was cut again. An inconvenience, really, but I understand why they did it. Hell, we did it too, when we found it. Water is valuable now; can't blame them for jumping at the chance to have their own.

Gabriel is out to torch their wall. Not all of them, no, I wouldn't want them to leave. I just want the water back. They need to learn, dammit, they need to learn that there is an order here. Z has ultimate seniority, followed by us, then the crawlers, *then* them.

It's not like I didn't already warn them once, so stop giving me grief.

I just want our water back.

The Suit and the Blonde

A black suit, a little browned by the sun and frayed just slightly at the sleeve, walks a few feet across the cement and plaster room to a blonde. She is turned towards a wall, and is resting small hands on her waist, fidgeting slightly; the only indication that she's unnerved. The frayed sleeve lifts and touches her purposefully on the shoulder. *Sophia*, the suit says, and she turns. She looks up at the suit and her pale blue eyes are unreadable, her face pulled a little across her cheekbones, making her appear worried, unfed, or a miserable mix of the two. (And I can tell you—I know because I am the suit and because Sophia has been a roommate of mine for years—that it is indeed a miserable mix of hunger and worry.)

Come, sit, have sugar cube. I know she's worried about Gabriel. She shouldn't be. He's just across the hall, and it's certainly not the first time he's had to confront a Problem. She should just feel lucky that this Problem is just pesky neighbors and not a bigger Problem, like the Eyes, or the Ears. She drops her shoulders a little, and takes the sugar cube offer—I knew she would. No one would give that up, especially over a non-issue like a routine Problem Fixing. She still eats timidly, though, perhaps just a façade at this point so I don't question whether or not the sugar cube was indeed necessary. Presently, she is squirreling the cube between her small hands, holding them close to her mouth, and holding the cube in place between the split in her lip. It sits there, content to drizzle down her front teeth and gums as a granular sugar paste.

I'm a tad annoyed. Her harelip is hardly an issue, not compared to Jeffrey's and certainly not compared to mine. Gabriel, her lover, and the party currently across the hall, also has the slightest of Abnormalities. They are the gifted couple, or at least they think they are, as they are the closest to the Normals. She knows how to eat normally, mind you, she is just eating in this fashion so I'll pity her. Fat chance, blondie.

The cube is still dripping down her exposed gums when Gabriel walks in, unharmed. She looks relieved, but then quickly puts the remaining cube in her mouth before looking at me nervously. She knows I know I just wasted a sugar cube.

Dammit.

Pictures

What else can I tell you about us? Oh, here, how about these pictures? They're old, from the only camera we could find. Actually, half of the pictures here are from the original owner, I would assume. I don't know these people, but we've made up stories about them over the years. Like this one.

This is Carl. He is on his way to Terminal B, where he is employed. He has a wife, Melissa, and two young girls. They are twins, and an absolute joy! See how he is holding that briefcase? He's head of communications for his cubicle. He reports to an officer, who reports to a commander, who reports to the Ears; so Carl almost directly reports to the Ears! He is important at work, but at home, he reports only to his wife.

And here, this is Babette. She is a beautiful model, and a spy for the Eyes. Watch out for her! She might just get someone like us!

This one is a little blurry, and the finger belongs to the cameraman. This is of his son, Bernard. Bernard is an aspiring officer, and has a collection of old time baseball cards. He also has a fascination of Abnormals from the twenty first century, back before they were outlawed. Right now, his favorite picture is of a burn victim. He just loves looking at those scars and knowing that he is better, both legally and morally. He's going to make a good officer someday.

You don't need to see these; these are just pictures of junk. If you're interested, I'll show them to you another time. But we're just getting to us, and I'm excited to show you!

Here's a picture of Sophia; you already know her. She doesn't like this picture, because we caught her while she was dripping. She hates that; sometimes, her lip spouts just like a faucet and runs down her chin. Nothing she can really do about it either, except wait it out or hold a towel under it.

And this is Gabriel. He's normal; at least on the outside. It just looks like he's shouting here, and he is. It's one of his fits, captured forever on camera. I think, if I remember correctly, that he was going about the Eyes when the episode started.

This one's of Jeffrey. He is beautiful, don't you think? Not sure why he's hanging out by the ceiling, but he's up there, just floating. I like Jeffrey the best out of all the roommates. The buzzing gets annoying at times, though. The beautiful bastard buzzes like a damn refrigerator when he floats around like that.

And this one's me. I haven't let you see it yet, but see how there's a little bit of light peeking out from my mouth? It bubbles out like that from time to time. I have to press my lips together like that to keep it in, but sometimes it gets too big and spills out. That's why I'm here; I don't even know when it's coming, and that would surely get me in trouble

with the Eyes. I didn't let them get a
real good picture of it, but I'll show you
right now if you want to see it. Just give
me a second, I've got to tease it up.

The List

Knox put the pictures back down in their haphazard pile, and walked towards the lovers who were holding each other and cooing. His suit was starched just a little too stiff, which made him look boxy. Gabriel put his hand up to Sophia's face and pushed her away slightly so he could face Knox.

"They said they'd put the pipe back, and I didn't have to torch the whole thing first. I think they're gonna be easier to live with than the crawlers."

Knox looked pleased.

"You know she got a sugar cube because she wouldn't calm down? I told her it was just a routine Problem, but she was just too worried. I'd have given you the cube, but I gave it to her instead."

At this, Gabriel turned towards the blonde, who was looking at him apologetically and nervously. He went to talk, but got up instead and moved to the other couch. The cube should have been his, and she knew it. From his new location, he spoke.

"Where is Jeffrey?"

"Kitchen, I believe, digging at the wall again."

Indeed, Jeffrey was several feet away, behind the refrigerator in the kitchen burrowing furiously into the wall; a newer hole that he'd only been working on for a few days. Older, deeper holes were scattered throughout the rest of the kitchen, abandoned for whatever reason. A few of the very old holes were plastered over, and one was half filled. It was pointless to fill them at this point.

"Hey, Jeffrey, why don't you leave that alone for a bit and come over here? We have to make the list."

There was a momentary silence, then a small crashing noise as Jeffrey dropped to the ground and walked into the living room where the other roommates were gathered.

"More spoons." His voice was meek and beautiful.

Sophia's eyes flit from Knox and Gabriel, and she held her pen close to a small scrap of paper.

"Jeffrey," Knox began, soothingly, convincingly, "I don't think we need any more spoons. We can try to find you something else to dig with, but let's not waste any room on the list this week, ok?"

The boy's angelic face dropped, but he had known that he wasn't getting more spoons long before he asked for them.

Sophia pulled the pen away from the paper.

"Maybe we can get a tin of jelly? Or butter? Not every week, but it might be nice to have it for just one or two weeks…" Her voice trailed off and she tried to melt into the wall.

Both Knox and Gabriel nodded, though, and she looked reassured. The pen scribbled against the scrap.

"And add paper, and a new pen, and bread rolls, and maybe one or two lines of pipe. And that's it, I think." Gabriel finished off the list and licked his lower lip.

Knox, breaking from his usually sure stance and tone, pulled a finger up to his eye and fiddled with invisible debris. His palm slightly covered his mouth as he spoke.

"Oh, also add Oxymorphin."

It didn't slide in effortlessly as he had intended.

The other three roommates looked up to him, and Sophia's pen wavered above the paper. A slight, persistent buzzing began from the general direction of Jeffrey. It grew and roiled and filled the silence until his feet left the floor and he began rising towards the low ceiling. He kept rising until his head had to twist half to the side to fit the rest of his body in the air. The buzzing reverberated in the small room. Knox looked embarrassed, and hung his head slightly down and to the left, avoiding the others' gaze.

Gabriel was visibly aggravated.

"Oxymorphin? You've gone and upset Jeffrey. Jeffrey, come on down. Come on, easy."

Jeffrey lowered until he stood on his toes. The buzzing died down only slightly.

"Look, Knox, why in the hell do you want Oxymorphin? You know what it does, you've seen what it can do."

Knox puffed up his chest with a deep breath, then spoke.

"I was thinking about trying to go out to get a job—I, I think it would be alright if I could get some of it. You know, it's, I don't want to be stuck with the list every week. Maybe, maybe if I could go outside with the Normals and get a small job we wouldn't have to."

His words hung in the air.

And wouldn't budge.

Sophia, sensing that the words were becoming too large and were starting to eat everyone, finally spoke.

"Maybe we could get jelly more often…. That might be nice."

Knox smiled just slightly. Gabriel snorted. And Jeffrey rose once more, drifting back towards the kitchen, knocking his head against the door molding as he passed.

Oxymorphin

He's just afraid, is all. You see,
Jeffrey was on the O not too long ago.
It was great, at least for while—O just
has this way with some people. One
day, he was walking around just fine,
and we all tried our hardest to get him
to lift. We tried scaring him, pissing
him off, making him happy, anything,
but nothing worked. Which means the
O was working. Honestly, for the first
time since I left home, I was hopeful.
And honestly, that was kind of a
frightening thing. To be hopeful after

being so desolate for so long. The others must have felt the same way too (maybe not Sophia, actually, now that I think about her specific condition, but definitely the rest of us.) For that one week, we could be Normals. And we could leave the Annex. The mill. Our quarantine.

Now sure, right about now you're thinking, *hey, Knox, so what was the problem? Why are you still there if you can be a Normal?*

I'm getting to that.

For that one week, even though three of us never took the O, and even though we never left the mill, we *were* Normals. We put things on the list that we didn't need. Things like soap. Or blankets. Or a bottle of whiskey. We lived like kings that week, dammit, because we could afford to. Or we thought we could afford to. 'Gone with the list!' 'Gone with the mill!' Our victory cries. We all wept. I wept. I let light bubble out all over the floor, and I didn't even bother to try to keep it in. Gabriel let the fits take over, and he cussed out the Eyes, and the Ears, and the Brain. Out of control, we were. You have to understand the significance this drug had on us. You have to understand; after living like rats for so long, and to have a chance to live like a human, to be able to walk on the streets with the Normals and not fear abduction by the Eyes. It was ecstasy. Better that, actually, because this high lasted an entire week.

But it only lasted for a week.

By the end of the day, on the seventh day of treatment, Jeffrey was a sight, to be sure. He had curled himself up in a corner and was oozing white froth from every hole in his body. We had to get buckets to clean the stuff up. Threw it in the grass outside and it damn near killed all the grass under it. And he went on like he had Gabriel's fits; mumbling and gurgling and snorting and arguing with no one present. He was mad, barking mad, and we were scared.

We didn't want to think that it was the Oxymorphin at first. Or at second, or third. We didn't want to give our high up just yet. So we kept on giving pretty Jeffrey the pills until one night Gabriel woke up to a demented Jeffrey aiming to gnaw his hand off. He'd made it quite far, mangling Gabe's hand pretty bad, and getting blood and the like all over his face and dripping down his chin. So he screamed, like anyone would, and I startled up, saw Gabriel, saw his face, saw his hand, then saw Jeffrey. (It was all pretty instantaneous, I probably didn't see it exactly in that order, but that's how I've figured it since then.)

Then I found myself in a bit of a situation; I certainly had not ever expected something like that to happen, and I had no inkling of an idea of how to go about fixing the problem. I'm pretty sure time slowed then, because I know I thought about at least a hundred things, several of which concerned how to go about getting this mad Jeffrey off Gabriel, and several of which concerned things like, 'what if he gets me?' 'have I said everything I want to say to whom I want to say it?' and even more simply, 'fuck, fuck, fuck, fuck!'

I don't think I actually ever decided on a course of action, my legs just kind of took control and threw me towards the beautiful, ravenous man, and all the while my head was going, 'No! Stop! Bad idea, bad idea!' but then my hands shot out, and I knocked hard into Jeffrey's stomach, and as soon as I did, he started spouting black foam like a hose, and his mouth opened wider and emptied the contents of his entire body until there was a big sickly puddle of sticky Jeffrey all over the floor.

And floating in the mess were ten little white pills, stamped with a perfect O.

The Maze

Paper, and a new pen, and bread rolls, and one or two lines of pipe, and no spoons, and Oxymorphin.

The list this week was only slightly longer than it had been in weeks prior. A starched box arm tucked into my starched box chest, hiding away the scrap of paper. The door to the main hall was thick metal, but rust and dents gave way to ragged holes. This was a door for keeping people out, and for keeping people in.

I made sure to close the door carefully. The neighbors were fine, sometimes, but the door wasn't put in its place for them anyway.

The Annex, the mill, home, and everything else that we called it, was not a place intended for living. The halls were blackened almost entirely, lit only by dusty cracks of sun that snuck in through broken walls and brick. The sun was tricky like that, here. Most of us would have preferred that it just go away, that it stop bothering itself with our derelict home. Instead of guiding us with a shining beacon, it sliced haphazardly through the perfect darkness, making it, in fact, harder to see. The hall was a maze of walls, some real, most not. Walk out the door, *bang* a wall. A hard wall. Quick turn left, three steps, *bang* another wall. You go right through this one, but you're blinded by the harsh light. Two steps *bang* another wall, you go through this one too. Five or six of these, then *bang* a hard wall. The edge of the mill. A left, a crumbling hard wall, step over it. *Bang* light, *bang* stairs. A rusted metal tetanus breeding ground of a door at the bottom of the stairs. This one is stuck shut, you think. It's not. Feel to the right. Feel that wire? Pull that. A click. Place your hand at the top of the metal and run it down slowly. Feel for the hole that's just big enough for your hand to fit through. Now fit it through. Reach down, two inches to the left. Pull that hook. Now push with all of your weight against your side of the door. See? It opens just fine.

Immediate right. Don't go in that room, the Crawlers are in there. Keep

going, quite though. They'll come out if
they hear you. Hassel you. Don't make
deals with the Crawlers. There's a wire
hanging from the ceiling right ahead.
Stop there, and move the wooden board
that's leaning against the hard wall
aside. Step through that, and follow the
stairs. Forty stairs to the bottom, quick
right, open the door (this one's like a
normal door you'd find anywhere else,
just turn the knob). Quietly, step to the
main door four feet ahead. Turn
sideways, and tuck yourself into the
crevice there. Now wait. Cynthia will
be here soon.

I wait.

Cynthia

She's old and she exudes smoke
and disease. Well, not old, but haggard.
She could be fifty. Or forty. Or twenty-
five. She's that type.

In a second, she's going to talk to
me. It must be difficult to talk with so
many rocks down her throat. I won't
make her talk much.

"You got a list ready?"

She doesn't know my name.

"Yes." It's sitting in my coat
pocket, crumpled a little along the

edges, so I pull it out for her and smooth it out.

"Paper, pen, rolls, piping…" The rocks are grinding against each other, and I wish she'd stop. "I have some of this now, if you have cash. Paper and rolls… three sheets, I think, and five rolls."

She doesn't wait for me to say I want them now. She's already sifting through her canvas sack for our listed items. As it turns out, I do want them. I pull out the cash I have on me.

"Alright. I'll have the pens and piping in next week."

She gets ready to leave, but her lazy eye is snagged on the last item on the list.

"Ox… you want Oxymorphin? The drug?"

I figure that's a rhetorical question, so I don't answer.

"This is dangerous shit, you know," she's visibly agitated, she doesn't want to be caught carrying Oxymorphin. That would certainly warrant an investigation by the Eyes. Normals don't have much need for Oxymorphin, except for kicks. And that trend died out a few years back. Sure, a few kids down the pills for a trip, but nowadays, its main market is the Abnormals. Yes, that would definitely warrant an investigation.

"I'll get it for you. Yeah, yeah, sure I'll get it for you. But I need double for it. I don't wanna carry that shit around. And you gotta be ready to pick up tomorrow. I *don't* wanna carry that shit around."

This will work for me.

"Pens and piping, too?"

"Yeah, yeah, sure. Pens and piping too."

Becoming Abnormal

The first few times navigating through the mill are difficult, for sure. I've made the trip to give Cynthia the list so many times now— once a week, several times a week— that it is now just second nature. I can do it with my eyes closed, if I want to. Sometimes I do. (Today, for example, I did.)

I've lost track of how long I've lived here. I think all of us have. None of us have a choice though, really. We are condemned here in the abandoned mill. We cannot ever let the Eyes see us or the Ears hear us. We live, more or less, like small rats and other unwanted vermin live in the walls of a house. We stay in when there is even the slightest chance that we will be spotted, unless we are suicidal, or fast enough to out run the host of our place of dwelling— and if we're fast enough, we also have to be sneaky enough to get back into our homes without them following us back or suspecting that we live where we live (because there's a larger rat population there, you know, and if you fuck it up, you've essentially given up the hiding place of all the other rats in your area.) I don't suggest risking it. The Eyes are hired and trained to be able to follow the vermin back to their hiding spots, which is good for the Normals, but pretty bad for us.

You must be looking at this place disdainfully. *There are no lights in the hallways; there aren't even real doors sometimes, everything is rusted and falling apart!* I don't see it that way anymore, this is my home now, and this place is safe. But I can understand where you are coming from (I apologize that you are stuck here with me now, by the way), because I was just like you when I first found the abandoned mills. I used to live in a home, you know. A real home with a locking door and windows and blood relation family.

I was little, and I lived with my mom. I probably had a father at some point, but I never met him, and my mother never talked about him. As far as I know, I was the only child. My mom treated me like I was, anyway. My mom— I'm just remembering this now, I hope that I don't ramble— was

quite fond of the American 1950's.
Never one for our time. Our house was
modeled after the little homes, and she
wore her hair neat and dressed herself
in the modest, structured dresses and
prints of the time. We even had one of
the white picket fences, and a small
kiddy pool in the back yard that we'd
fill up with the hose in the summer
when you needed something wet and
cool to keep from exploding. Anyway,
it was summer, so that pool was filled,
and I was sitting in it, pruning slowly
and watching my mom cook over the
old fashioned grill we had. She was
wearing a white dress, with a high
neckline and little printed flowers. And
I was just sitting there in the cool water,
kicking around a little to keep it from
stagnating.

"A hot dog, Knox?" Her voice was a bell that cut through the heavy air.

I went to talk, but stopped. Instead of words, a thick bile was rising up my throat and towards my mouth. There was no way that I was going to let myself be sick in the kiddy pool, because I didn't want to stew in my own vomit for the rest of the day, so I closed my lips tight and tried to swallow it back down. It worked for less than a second, then it was back, and pushing hard against the inside of my mouth. It wanted to get out, I'm sure, and I can't really blame it. It was hot, and it probably just wanted to enjoy the cool water too. *A hot dog, bile?* No, it wasn't going to come out on my watch. So despite the increasing pressure and bubbling going on behind my lips, I kept them closed tight.

My mother had stopped cooking. She looked frozen, almost like a statue, and her eyes were fixed on the fence. She was even shaking a little, I think, but I didn't pick up on that at the time.

"Knox…" she began. Perhaps she was going to tell me to go in the house, perhaps she was going to tell me that she loved me, perhaps she was going to tell me to run and hide. Or perhaps she was just going to ask again if I wanted a hot dog, since I hadn't answered her the first time she asked. In any case, she didn't have a chance to finish, because right as she said my name, our fence splintered away and was plowed down by twenty men in official uniform. Each man wore a glass mask that covered their features and reflected exactly what was in front of them, so that when they were facing you to take you away, you'd only see yourself, and you'd know exactly why they were hauling you away, and that it was nobody's fault but your own for being so abnormal.

Each uniform had a patch that stared at you with a cold, unblinking fabric eye.

They had our yard surrounded immediately, and I'm sure my mother must have been regretting the white picket fence then. There was no way for either of us to escape, even if there had only been one or two of the uniformed men. This was, I realize, the beginning of the trend of being like a rat, as I was metaphorically trapped like one.

Keep in mind, I was still a little fellow, and any sort of situation in which a large group of men break down your walls and surround you suddenly is bound to be more than a little stressful, if not terrifying. This did not help with the bile situation. In fact, it made it much, much worse, and it started roiling and bubbling big, fat, bubbles that were increasingly more difficult to fit behind my closed lips. My mouth was as stretched as it could possibly be, and I was just able to keep my lips touching.

I kept them together until one bubble was just a millimeter bigger, and managed to pry them open. Relief was immediate, as it poured out of me and into the kiddy pool, filling it to the brim then spilling over, but my mother was screaming and the uniforms rushed the little Knox. I was walled in by mirrors completely, as if I was in a fun house, and it was only then that I stopped to look at what was coming out

of my mouth. Not bile, but light.
Gushing, thick, bubbling light, like a
liquid metal, reflected in the mirrors
and completely blinding me. Blinding
them too, apparently, because somehow
I managed to jump out of the pool and
break through the wall of mirrors. I ran
towards my mother's white dress and in
one movement she lifted me and got me
over the fence. They shot her, and I felt
her hand fall from under my back, but I
was already over the fence and I ran.

And I ran, and I ran, and I didn't
stop until I was at a run down and
abandoned mill.

Then I cried.

Safety Precautions

I met Cynthia exactly as I had the day before; same spot, same time. And as expected, at exactly the same time she had yesterday, the haggard woman knocked once then opened the back entrance to the Annex and stepped inside.

I stepped out from the crevice near the door, money already in hand, and hand resting loosely in my coat pocket.

"Pens and piping," she said, handing them over.

I noticed that there was grime on her fingers, and didn't much care to touch them. In order to avoid contact, I grabbed the pens at the tip and grabbed the piping close to the end. She didn't notice, or maybe she just didn't care (maybe, also, she didn't want to touch an Abnormal. In that case, I wouldn't feel bad about not wanting to touch her hands. A mutual distaste is not nearly as offensive.) She shoved the grimy hand quickly into her canvas sack (which, as a side note, was also considerably dirty), and felt around for a moment. She hit something that made the sound of a rattle, and she must have grabbed that object, because it continued to rattle up and out of the bag.

"The Oxymorphin." She half whispered this, and I think this helped stop the rocks in her throat from grinding together. Not completely though.

You could tell that she was anxious to get out of the mill, so I indulged her that and quickly handed her the money. She turned to leave, hesitated, then turned back around to face me.

"I'd say you should take that pretty quick. There was an Officer hanging around the corner on my way over… he didn't see me, I'm sure, but he's out there. Just so you know."

Then she left.

~~~

My roommates were not thrilled with this news, and suggested that we not purchase anything through the list system for a while. The less the mill was trafficked, even if by a seasoned professional like Cynthia, the better. Of course, this meant calling a meeting of the rest of the mill. We don't interact much with the other groups, but when something like this happens, we have to tell them. Even if we didn't care to look out for them, we'd still have to tell them so that they would cut off contact with Cynthia too. The mill had a built in safety net that way.

Gabriel and Sophia discussed the logistics of the meeting— Jeffrey, although clearly affected by the news of a possible Eye investigation, remained too concerned with the growing hole in the wall of the kitchen to join the discussion. I was too distracted by the bottle of pills rattling around in my pocket. Gabriel stopped, just once and only briefly, to look down at my pocket. Sophia followed his gaze, but was not nearly as troubled or passive as her lover was. In truth, I was worried about the pills as well. I knew, perhaps better than anyone, the consequences that I was subjecting myself to. But I also *saw* more than anyone the growing discontent of the Annex; everyone, not only myself, was becoming restless after years of voluntary confinement. Everyone in the Annex needed this opportunity just as much as I did.

And I had no problem testing our future.

My hand was resting in my coat pocket, and I had my fingers wrapped carefully around the bottle. Every so often, I would turn it around once to hear the clicking of the tabs against one another. I needed to remind myself that they were there, and I was mesmerized. My thoughts would drift: *Oxymorphin, I have Oxymorphin in my pocket* right now; *I'll be normal, for once; I'll be*

*able to get a job, imagine that, I can get
a job and we can get whatever we'd
like every week, hell, we could leave the
mill entirely, and we could buy our own
shit; no, I'm going to end up exactly
like Jeffrey did, I'm going to go bat shit
and kill somebody; they're gonna have
to put me down; Sophia won't be able
to watch, and it will be Gabriel that
does it; he'll say, "goddammit, O was a
bad idea, it was a bad idea and I told
him, and now I have to kill him;" I
wonder if I'll fight back, I wonder if I'd
kill Gabriel, because he'd be right, you
know, he'd be right and I would have
been wrong all along.* Turn.
*Oxymorphin, I have Oxymorphin in my
pocket* right now…

Gabriel touched my shoulder.

"Knox," he must have already said
my name a few times.

"Knox, we're calling a meeting. Now."

The Meeting

Mill meetings are a rarity. They are simply never called, for any reason. Only once before have I been summoned, and that was in the beginning, back when it was just me and Z in the mill.

We have drills, sometimes, to make sure that everyone knows where to go and what to do. Like a fire drill in a Normal's children's school. Just to get the basics down. 'Get to the midway, remove the mallet and tap the piping repeatedly and with force.' There was no room in the abandoned mill that could not hear the piping when it was struck.

This time, though, was not a drill. Gabriel and Sophia pulled Jeffrey from his spot in the kitchen and brought him to the hall. Jeffrey would not be making any significant contributions to today's discussion, but he had to be present. It was in the rules; all occupants, regardless of status (meaning even during an episode of Abnormality) must show up at a called meeting. Prevents sabotages and territory wars that way.

The midway is the easiest spot to find in the entire mill, for ease of access. It is simply an open area on the second floor (directly in the middle of the building on all sides, for ease of location, but also for security reasons) that has a long unused and inactive water main running from the first floor to the roof. All pipelines stem from this main line; some are functional, others aren't; but all pipes resonate with the harsh metal sounds of a summoning bell.

As during every drill, I struck the pipeline hard with the mallet hanging on the wall. When you're in the midway, the volume is unbearable, and even Jeffrey snapped out of his haze to look around wildly and cover his ears. The others showed up quickly; there hadn't been a scheduled drill. There was a clear panic on all fronts.

The Crawlers, who arrived at the mill shortly after I did, made their way in first. In typical Crawler fashion, they stayed low to the ground and close to the walls; they were a distrusting people, with no Abnormalities immediately visible. Generally a sign of an extremely dangerous Abnormality. Twisted sickos and murderous thieves were the types without visible ailments… we left the Crawlers alone whenever possible.

The New Tenants, as we had taken to calling them, arrived next. You will remember that we had just recently torched one of their walls— clearly, they would not be enthused to spend time with us. (Actually, I'm quite surprised that they showed up at all regardless of the fact; they have only been in the mill for a few months, and I don't recall any drill meetings since they moved in.) Gabriel especially tensed up when they walked in to the room. Naturally, Sophia became agitated when she saw her lover's reaction. For a split moment I was more concerned with the presence of the New Tenants than I was with the Crawlers. But only for an instant.

They would all be on their best behavior today, though. Everyone was on edge; no one knew exactly why they were summoned.

Gabriel, who had decided to call the meeting, and who had been elected to head the meeting, looked to me now. He was uncomfortable around the New Tenants, and he didn't want his Abnormality to flare up. (Flare-ups, you see, are discomforting during meetings; no one wants to be the first or the only to have an uncontrolled episode in front of another group.) I indulged him this.

"I'm going to get straight to the point, I'm sure you won't mind; none of us want to be here and I don't want to keep anyone here for any longer than we have to. The mill is being watched."

A dull panicked buzzing sounded throughout the room, echoing off the walls.

"At least we think it is. Cynthia, of trades, informed me earlier this morning that see saw an Eye snooping around the block. Now, he may very well be investigating another area, or he may have just been making rounds, but the fact is, he is in the area. For that reason, my room has decided to forgo all purchases and list services for the time being. We suggest, we *implore* you to do the same."

I looked around to all of the other tenants, then continued.

"The less traffic comes through to the mill, the better. We don't want what may be a routine round to become a full blown investigation."

There was a silence, then one of the New Tenants spoke.

"Why are they investigating the mill? This is a safe place, who fucked it up and blew the cover?"

His bulbous eyes wandered from me to Gabriel, still obviously sore over the wall and pipe situation.

"No one in this mill is stupid enough to blow the cover."
Gabriel is not stupid enough to blow the cover.

"You stole our water line, and we took appropriate action. We do not have any fundamental problems with you or your group, and we are certainly not willing to put *our* safety in jeopardy to inconvenience you."

A few of the Crawlers looked over at the New Tenants distastefully. Even the Crawlers follow certain simple etiquette rules in the mill, one of which frowns upon stealing a necessity such as water. In truth and in practice, anything goes here, including theft of furniture, supplies, space... we do not touch food or water, though.

The New Tenant did not speak. Instead, a Crawler turned to address him.

"How we know it wasn't be you that gone and blew the cover?"

His words, like the rest of his character, slunk to the floor and writhed around until they came to the New Tenant. They stopped at his feet and twisted their way slowly, methodically, up his leg. The sinewy words continued creeping up until they danced grossly in front of his face, then slipped into his ear.

Again, the New Tenant stood speechless, fish mouth open and gaping. With his eyes downcast, he melted into the floor and blended with the wall.

"So do we have an agreement? Everyone cuts off contact with Cynthia and any other passers through?"

All eyes shifted towards the New Tenant that was slowly being absorbed by the wall. When he did not object, I proceeded.

"Alright. We will not leave a note for Cynthia, it is far too risky. As she was the one who notified me of their presence, she will surely understand its absence, and will, perhaps, expect it. For now, we ask that everyone lie low."

I stopped, ready to return to the familiar comfort of the Annex. Jeffrey was looking at me with a lucidity that had been absent for months, brows furrowed. Sophia's porcelain hands shook with a delicate tremor.

I turned back to the tenants.

"Obviously, none of us can risk an investigation."

Nobody made a move to leave for a thousand years; everybody wanted to stay in the midway safe pocket, disconnected from the lives they were now afraid to live and disconnected from the Eyes that made them so afraid.

The Last Supper

The mill has a rodent problem. They are everywhere, they infiltrate every damn room in the mill. If the Eyes ever managed to train rats for searches, we would be screwed, to say the least.

The mill rats are especially adjusted to human life, they tend to stay out of our way (especially now a days since food is running low), but are not afraid of us the way animals from the outside tend to be. For a while, before taking Oxymorphin, Jeffrey befriended one of

the mill rats. The damn thing kept
showing up right at his feet when we
had our rolls, every night, religiously,
hoping for a crumb, or whatever. Of
course, we never really produced too
many crumbs; when you only get to eat
one roll every day or two, you are very
careful to not drop anything.

But I digress.

This rat kept showing up, probably
for a few months, and one night Jeffrey
ripped off a chunk of his roll and
dropped it to the floor. Sophia's doll
eyes bulged out, and she grabbed at it
hysterically, but he stepped hard on her
fingers, pinning her far away from the
large crumb. The rat, obviously
surprised at the gift, nabbed it and ate it
quickly as if he was afraid that Jeffrey
would steal it back or crush him. The
rat waited there after he finished that

crumb, but Jeffrey didn't drop any more bread that night. The rat was around constantly after that though, hanging at Jeffrey's feet and following him from room to room. He just wanted food, I think, but Jeffrey was sure that it just liked being around him. Jeffrey would spend his time talking to it, and holding it, and made the damn thing near domestic.

We weren't displeased, though. Gabriel always had Sophia, I was always busy dealing with mill relations or general upkeep, and that left Jeffrey alone for most of the day. That probably got to him, I mean, I always considered Jeffrey my closest and most dear friend at the mill, but that little guy probably needed more companionship than I could give him. Anyway, we didn't mind this rat; not at all.

Jeffrey ended up eating him one night when he was on O.

The Old Jeffrey never fully came back after the bad trip, but he did wonder where his rat had gone.

Gabriel wanted to leave the bones and bloody mess of a rat on the floor for Jeffrey to find on his own; he was still bitter. Sophia moved it though, and I cleaned up the stain. We told him we had no idea where the rat went, and that maybe one of the Crawlers was giving it food now.

Tonight, as Sophia portioned out the last of our bread rolls, several rats showed up looking for crumbs. Jeffrey's did not.

~~~

"Knox.." I looked to Sophia, who was running her tongue over the pink space between her split lip. The doll eyes peeked over to Gabriel, who was attentively watching the fragile girl, apparently interested in what she was preparing to say.

"Knox, we're out of rolls."

How much so few words can say. Gabriel muscled his jaw to a set close, the ropey muscle quivering from under his skin. Sophia's small tongue darted out to moisten the gums again.

In five words, she told me that we had run out of food, but she had also asked me how we were going to solve this dilemma now that we didn't have the list service.

She was asking me to find a way to feed our make shift family, to get a job or find some other means that would get us bread.

She was asking me to become a normal, to take O; to betray and go against the wishes of her lover.

And in five words, she avoided all conflict with him.

"I know."

And in two words, I calmed her and sent Gabriel into a silent rage.

The rest of dinner was tense. Gabriel ate in silence, shifted slightly away from me and from Sophia; waves of anger and disapproval rolled off of him almost visibly. Sophia, in reaction to Gabriel, ate slowly and squirrel like, not eating fast enough to finish first, but not eating so slow that she wouldn't feel the effects of the only remaining food. And Jeffrey buzzed in the kitchen, digging away at the wall incessantly, ignoring our calls to dinner, and looking ahead with glazed eyes as we all in turn tried to offer him his roll. Later he grabbed a handful of loose plaster from the walls and ate it hurriedly; Jeffrey buzzed in the kitchen, a reminder of the dangers of O. Dinner was a silent affair that spoke to the division of our family.

Gabriel finished his first, and went straight to his mattress pad. He wanted to fall into sleep and leave all of us behind. I wanted him to do that, too. I could do what I had to do (*turn*) with him oblivious in dream.

Tonight, for the first time in years, Sophia did not follow him to bed. Another blow, even one this significant, wouldn't make their situation drastically worse. Instead, she followed me to the window.

My hand wandered into the stiff pockets of my coat, immediately touching the pills and sounding the rattling of our future. It was a comfort for me now, after holding them and handling them all day, but it rattled Sophia. I knew she was remembering Jeffrey, and his bloody chin. Remembering Gabriel. Picturing me.

I touched her lightly on the hand.

"I won't...I'm not Jeffrey, don't worry so much, Sophia. Trust me."

She turned away from me now, too.

"Sophia,"

I grabbed her shoulder to turn her around, but stopped at the puddle on the floor.

She turned back to me, saliva and tears dripping off her small chin. I wanted to pull her close as a comfort, but didn't. She was too small, too delicate, and would have shattered against my solid box suit.

Instead, I cupped my hands under her face, catching the dripping saliva.

"It's not going to be like Jeffrey. We will be ready this time. Sophia, you have to understand why this is important. Please tell me you understand."

She nodded, so I continued.

"I will get chains, okay? I'll lock myself up if things start to go bad. I won't hurt anybody, I promise."

She began to dry up, and spoke through a shallow pool of spit.

"Promise?" It was gargled.

I nodded, hoping to end her display. This was uncomfortable, and I was losing the patience to deal with her blubbering.

"But you have to promise me something too, okay?"

I was speaking to an infant.

"Don't let Gabriel stop me from taking it. Promise me you won't let me stop taking it either."

I realized this was vital, and began choking to get all of the words out in time.

"I need to know what happens, if Jeffrey's attack was just another passing stage. What happens next— just, please, Sophia…"

She was deathly white and completely silent. Motionless.

Then she nodded.

I placed one of the white pills on my tongue swallowed.

Day One

The pill went down hard without water.

Aside from that, the first pill was not an issue. It was a little smaller than a fingernail, perfectly white, perfectly round, and stamped with a perfect 'O'.

O for Oxymorphin.

O for Opportunity.

I didn't feel much right away, just a slight gurgling in my stomach.

It felt like the beginning of my episodes.

Only it wasn't.

I wondered how long it would take for the pill to work. I tried to tease up the light. I felt my stomach bubble, cramp up, then settle.

As far as I'm concerned, it was working marvelously.

Sophia was looking at me, worried. I smiled, and she lost all tension she was holding in her face and hands. She left to join Gabriel in their bed, and I followed closely behind, pausing only momentarily to see Jeffrey hovering and buzzing, digging away at the wall as if nothing else mattered. I lay flat on my mattress pad, and a nagging maggot of worry gnawed at the back of my neck. Only momentarily, though, then sleep curled its warm fingers around me and pulled me in to a deep, dreamless sleep.

Day Two

Gabriel and Sophia were already awake when I woke. I heard them talking in the kitchen, perhaps talking about my decision with Jeffrey, perhaps not.

My sleep had been deep, embryonic. Only for a moment was it disturbed by the colorful fingers of dream, pushing against the embryonic layer that enclosed me and surrounded me. They slipped against the smooth rubbery surface, unable to break through. Other than that, I slept in utter darkness and silence.

I got up out of the bed and made my way to the kitchen. *I should show them that I'm not loony yet,* I though. *Yet.* I was scared suddenly by that thought.

I had expected that Gabriel would be in a sour mood all day, perhaps for the next week up until I snapped, if I even snapped, so that he could be legitimately angry with me and say that he told me so. But he wasn't. He had his arms wrapped around Sophia and was laughing with her. Even Jeffrey had broken his impenetrable concentration to smile and stand on the floor. I was floored.

Sophia looked at me, quickly, perhaps she didn't even look at me at all it was so quick, and smiled only for me. She was holding the place down, taking my place, as it were, while I was on O. She was keeping the peace, and making life as easy for me as possible. I loved her at the moment. My ally.

"I'm going out for a job this morning. I'm going to get one as soon as possible so that we can start getting food again. I'll try to pick some up tonight."

Blunt, and to the point.

Gabriel broke his hold from Sophia and walked over to me.

"Alright, good, that's what this is all for, right? But you're not going outside the mill if you're not completely passable for a Normal, we need to find a way to test it."

This had to be a different Gabriel. But I conceded. Actually, it was a very good idea. I had tested the affects of the pill briefly last night, but I couldn't be totally sure that they were working. Testing was indeed a very good idea.

Gabriel asked me to open my mouth, all the while remaining perfectly still and silent. Then he screamed— bloodcurdling, long, and agonizing.

My bones rattled with the electric shock of sudden startle. Jeffrey was sent into a panicked buzz and Sophia doubled over in an onslaught of gushing saliva.

And Gabriel smiled.

"Alright. I think this might actually work."

I reached into my pocket (*turn*) and popped another O, just to be sure the effects wouldn't wear off before I had a chance to take them again tonight. Gabriel tensed up when I did this— as I had thought, he wasn't completely comfortable with the plan.

But he was tolerating it, which was more than I could have ever asked for. I walked towards the door to allow them to get back to their cajoling.

"Knox! Wait!"

A voice I hadn't heard in over a year.

Jeffrey.

He was on the floor and walked over to me. He looked me straight in the eyes, and for a moment, I thought I could see Old Jeffrey, the Jeffrey that had intelligent thoughts and ideas. And for a moment, I thought Old Jeffrey, or New Jeffrey, or whoever it was that I saw, wanted to tell me something impossibly important.

Instead, he hugged me.

~~~

I left through the hidden entrance to the mill so that I wouldn't be seen by any patrolling Eyes. The entrance began at flight of stairs accessible from all floors and let out in a small basement. A hole was dug out of the cement and lead to a pile of boarded up debris covered in vegetation outside the mill. The Eyes would not find this entrance among all of the other piles of rubble and debris surrounding the mill.

This passageway was a gift from Z, who had likely crafted it years before. He would have been careful to ensure it would not be visible.

The first thing I saw when I stepped out from the covered hole in the back lot was dirt. Lots of dirt; brown wet dirt; red dry dirt. I reached down and touched the brown dust--it stuck to my fingers. Dirt and dust coated everything unused in the mill, I'd seen plenty of dirt in my years there. But I had not seen Earth Dirt. I had not touched or smelled or tasted real dirt since I was a small boy. I could smell it, too. In fact, I could smell damn near everything: dirt, trees, flowers, cement, trash, leather, smoke, electronics, people, cars, metals, smells I hadn't smelled in years and that I'd almost nearly forgotten about entirely. The dirt felt soft and foreign under my feet, and the sun felt overly warm and dry on my skin. I basked in the warm light for a moment as I walked away from the mill; I had spend too long in the damp and dank air of the Annex. I couldn't walk right on the dirt and grass, and immediately sought out familiar surface: cement.

The second thing I noticed was the Normals.

They were everywhere; they polluted the streets, the sidewalks, the buildings, the televised billboards. It was terrifying, being surrounded by so many Normals. Each and every last one of the people that I was walking among would give me up to the Eyes if they could see that I was Abnormal. Looking at them now, I couldn't help but feel an animosity towards them; they were the reason we were forced into hiding, they were the reason I had to live the way I did; but oddly, I found myself intrigued by them, too. In their own ways, they were just as abnormal as us. They each had their own mannerisms, their own step, their own tick. I saw women that reminded me of

Sophia, men that reminded me of Gabriel and Jeffrey. And of myself.

I felt cheated, all of a sudden.

I continued down the sidewalk, noticing large steel and cement structures, Eyes and other Officers on nearly every corner, business men and business women; so very different from the 1950s world I was brought up in. Or maybe it wasn't. I didn't know for sure.

Flat television screens were mounted on every building, depicting only the Mouth, the spokesman for the Brain, e-nun-ci-a-ting every syllable of city mandates:

> Do not forget your copy of the Code Of Law when leaving your house in the morning.
> Please operate with regard to standard law.

Thank your Officers for their duty; report all suspected Abnormals to your districts Office.

Curfew tonight is set for 22:00.

Do not forget: Taxes are due next quarter!

Televised billboards displayed two sets of hands shaking in a deal; the brain, and some other government official, surely. Stores had perfect LED displays of their prices and sales. People walked in a chaotic but perfect order. Everyone had his or her place, and everyone was heading there steadily. It was thrilling to be a part of this system, even as an imposter.

I approached a store with a 'Help Wanted: Inquire Inside' display, pausing momentarily to look inside.

The outsider looking in. The Abnormal looking in on the Normal world.

Inside, a young child was holding a big yellow umbrella up to the counter, which was several inches above her golden head. She stood on her toes to bring her eyes level as her mother paid for the yellow thing. The girl had perfect yellow curls that bounced gently, naturally, in her pig tails. She wore black patent leather strap on shoes and a white dress. My mother's dress. It wasn't, of course, it wasn't the same style, and certainly not the same size, but I recognized the fabric and the fit. I couldn't take my eyes of the young girl— I was immediately kin to her when I saw that dress. How she wanted that yellow umbrella! She looked at it longingly, waiting as patiently as a young child can to possess this yellow thing.

The color matched her hair, I noticed. The mother made small talk with the clerk, neither too particularly interested in the conversation. Meanwhile, the girl was staring at the umbrella, fidgeting now, wishing her mother would just hurry up and pay the man so that she could hold her yellow umbrella! I was furious at the mother for a second; I wanted her to stop talking to the clerk, I wanted her to pay for the umbrella and hand it to the little girl, I wanted her to buy the little girl ice cream on the way home, then tuck her into bed (with the umbrella propped up against the wall so that she could see it if she wanted to.) But that was nonsense.

I walked inside and waited in line to talk to the clerk, to 'Inquire Inside.'

The clerk noticed me, and ended the conversation politely with the girl's mother. She finally handed the man her pay card and pulled the umbrella off the counter. She didn't hand it to the girl. Pigtails grabbed at it, rightfully, and my heart leapt for her when the mother handed it to her distractedly; she didn't understand the child's excitement for the yellow umbrella, but it was achingly important to the girl. I wanted to reach out and playfully rough up her yellow curls, but I didn't.

I left the store with a job as a window cleaner; my pay would be below minimal, but that was a small fortune for me and the rest of the mill. The man asked, 'Would you like to start today?' and I said, 'Why, yes, I suppose I could, if that is convenient for your company.' He said it was, and gave me a spray bottle and a cloth. I was elated, but hid it well.

I spend the rest of the day cleaning the windows. I cleaned the same spots over and over; they all seemed clean compared to the mill windows, even before I had started my daily work. There were no scratches, no opaque stains, or cracks, or caked on bugs, or layers of hardened dirt; these windows were spotless, but needed to be cleaned, apparently. I kept working, spraying the window with the spray bottle, wiping it off with the cloth, and repeating. The clerk eventually came outside, gave me an odd look, and told me they were closing for the night, and that I could go home. I said, 'Okay, thank you.' And he said, 'Yeah, sure.' He handed me my 3.50 for the day and put the spray bottle and now dripping cloth inside. Then he locked the store, and left. I stayed at the window, letting people pass me, holding the money in my pocket. 3.50. This would have paid for an entire months food in the list service, if we were still using it, but I knew that it would get significantly less out here.

I bought a full loaf of bread; it was soft, and was easily big enough to last us two days.

I also picked up a small jar of strawberry jam, mostly for Sophia, as she had wanted it before. And she deserved it, now. I needed a way to thank her.

After the bread and the jam, I had .30 left, so I picked up an apple as well.

We had never had fruit at the mill, and I had only a vague recollection of what it tasted like from when I was a child.

~~~

I took my time walking home. I didn't want to return to the damp and heavy air of the mill. I liked being outside, and for a moment forgot why I couldn't spend all of my time out there. (*Turn*). The pills rattled, though, and reminded me.

I reached the hidden entrance, careful to look out for Eyes patrolling the area, and moved the low growing vegetation to get back in to the small basement space. I turned once more to bid the outside farewell for the night, and I am thankful I did; as I turned, the now red sun caught my eye and lit up the sky with spectacular colors. Reds, pinks, oranges, purples, blues of every shade radiated out from the glowing red sun and faded to a dark blue night sky.

A sunset I hadn't seen clearly in many, many years.

My roommates were asleep by the time I got in. I felt for the day's payment in my coat pocket, and lay down on my bed, thankful (for the first time in a long time) for the thin comfort of a mattress pad.

Sleep swallowed me quickly.

~*~

Tonight, it manages to writhe its way into my dead sleep. Fingers, smoky wisps of color and shape, wrap themselves around my head and envelope my body. I'm floating; the world is being painted around me. Cerulean blue drips down from above and expands infinitely outward, and a muted brown blotches out under me. It's taking shape. A boat shape. I'm in a boat now? Okay, alright, I can do a boat. The blue keeps falling. The sky is under me now, above me. Where's the water? This is just sky. The boat is just about solid now, so I can walk to the edge to look for the water. Oh. There it is, about a thousand feet under me.

A spot next to me implodes in on itself, puckering at the seams. Shapes and colors of the world I left behind were reflected in the wound, and for a moment, I could have slipped through the hole and fallen onto a street side. The wound immediately begins scarring over, a silky white skin that's just a little bit pearled. It bubbles out and up and stretches and turns until its formed a little clay person shape, then that large sized blob shoots out sideways into many more clay person shapes. The fabric of the space around me heaves in, then out suddenly, and I'm completely surrounded by my boat and my crew.

Well.

Everyone is busy at work, and I'm just standing there. My feet are glued to the deck.

(Upon closer inspection, I discover that I'm not glued, but rather that a bit of the boat melded with the bottom of my foot, holding me in place.)

A large humpbacked fellow knocks into me, grunts, and continues forward on his trajectory. I want to follow him, he's wearing the captain's hat, and I go to move but I can't.

Oh, right, my foot is stuck in the boat.

It's certainly frustrating, to be stuck like this. I can't move on my own, and the bustling crew looks right on past me. I'm an infant, so I do what an infant would do: I reach my arms out in front of me and clench my fingers together repeatedly. *Pick me up, pick me up!*

That's the ticket. A short squat guy sees me and plucks me out of the boat.

By the time I'm freed, I almost forget why I wanted to move so badly. His feathered brim catches my eye, and I remember. It looks like he's busy manning the wheel, and no one else is minding him, but I want so badly to talk to him.

"Hello, good sir. Where is this fine vessel headed?"

He doesn't hear me for a moment, then turns his massive head towards me. It must weigh a thousand pounds, and it moves as if he's breaking some cement plastered bond between his neck and his head. Bits of old plaster tap on the deck as they fall from his skin.

He's not smiling, and he's quite ugly. His face is pocked and swollen, as if he's allergic to just about everything around him. It's kind of awkward to try to look him in the eyes; they're so swollen shut, I wonder if he can even see that I'm trying to be courteous.

Still looking (or perhaps not looking at all) at me, he reaches a grizzled hand up and plucks the hat right off his head and places it on mine. Then he leaves. No sounds, no instructions, just a slow shuffle step back towards the other crewmates that is staggered to accommodate the large lump in his back.

So I do what anyone would do. I grab the wheel and spin it wildly and without direction.

Day Three

I woke up.

Immediately the fog of sleep was lifted and I got up from the sagging mattress pad.

My bag of purchases was still tucked into my coat pocket; I could feel them.

I looked up for the first time; Gabriel and Sophia were sitting on their mattress, looking towards me not with fear, but with trepidation.

"What?"

They both jumped slightly, startled.

"You're up."

It was a statement.

I turned to Gabriel, "Yes."

I'm not sure what else he wanted from me. No, I'm not crazy. No, I didn't forget to bring back food. Yes, I'll get to it in a second, I'm just now waking up.

"It is all in my pocket. Give me a second. Where's Jeffrey?"

They both looked relieved. I spoke to them, and rationally; I wasn't dangerous yet. Gabriel pointed to the kitchen, of course. Oh, Jeffrey.

I should probably give them the food. They are getting restless. I thought.

I leaned backwards slightly and cracked my back; the mattress was not the most comfortable, and after walking and cleaning windows all day yesterday, my back was more stressed than usual. Both of them noticed. Sophia looked concerned and I knew she'd offer to try to fix it. But not around Gabriel. For now, she would keep her arms around him and keep her head on his shoulder; his sheep. She wouldn't talk. She wouldn't think. Decisions were for Gabriel.

"Here, I was able to pick bread and the jam you had wanted, and I had money left over for an apple as well. The bread is soft. Touch it."

Both of my roommates stared open mouthed at my purchases. Neither had seen fresh bread in years, let alone jam. They had probably never tasted an apple either.

"Go ahead, you can touch it. It will probably stay soft for a few days too. I'll be able to pick up more before then, if you want that over something else."

Gabriel reached out for the lump of bread. His hand wavered over it, not wanting to touch it, or perhaps savoring the moment and committing it to memory. Then, slowly and deliberately, he poked the bread with his pointer finger. It hit the crust with a gentle thud then sunk in slowly; a down feather pillow being compressed at a single point. He licked his lips in a daze.

"Sophia, he was serious. It's soft. Touch it."

With his permission, Sophia unwrapped a slender arm from Gabriel and reached for the bread. She pushed down carefully with three fingers and gaped at the flexibility.

She looked back at Gabriel in awe. He smiled at her, just as pleased himself. I had impressed them with my first days work. I would be allowed to keep taking O.

"Get Jeffrey in here. Let him see it."

I wanted Jeffrey to experience this too. He had, after all, been the first and the bravest in venturing into O. He was the pioneer— that he couldn't keep on it was no fault of his own. I had more respect for Jeffrey, surely, than any of the other roommates. He was my inspiration, and my warning.

Sophia rose gracefully from the bed and went into the kitchen. Gabriel stared after her, as did I, as we waited for Jeffrey to enter the room. (It had been several weeks since Jeffrey slept in the bedroom with us. On any given night, he would be up digging away at the wall, always creating new holes or expanding old ones. I only saw him stop to sleep on occasion; I would find him curled up in the corner of the kitchen or floating up against the ceiling in a buzzing haze.)

She entered with Jeffrey in tow. He was loosely holding her fingers and staring bewildered at the room, and at us. He looked directly at me, and my spine tingled. Moments of the Old Jeffrey were unnerving.

"Jeffrey, touch this, its bread I picked up yesterday. The pills worked, so far, and I have a job cleaning windows," I said, offering him the loaf.

Gabriel and Sophia looked at me, now. I had not told them what I had gotten as a job. I think they were slightly envious that I had chosen to share this with Jeffrey first. He was just a mindless mass of human form in their eyes; the retarded brother that had to be kept safe. But he wasn't, and I knew that. He was our Jeffrey, our buzzing angel. He was only the way he was because he had wanted to help us.

Jeffrey reached out without the hesitation that the others had shown. He grabbed the bread and squeezed it in a fist, before bringing it quickly to his mouth and devouring a large chunk.

Sophia gasped.

Gabriel jumped up and snatched the bread away from him.

Jeffrey was content with his chunk of bread, and although the others were upset with him, and dismayed that a good sized chunk of bread was missing. I was elated; Jeffrey, too, approved of my endeavors.

Jeffrey looked to Gabriel, slightly afraid and mostly ashamed, then floated back to the kitchen. Within moments, we heard the picking and falling of plaster.

"Gabriel, it's alright. He can have as much as he wants. I can get this much bread every day. It's not an issue."

He wouldn't give in, and looked angered.

"He cannot just go around eating new food like that. We have to portion our food. Save it. We cant be buying bread every day. We need to be saving for bigger things. Better things."

"You're right. We will be saving for better things. But Gabe, please, we don't have to ration food anymore."

On a second thought, I added, "and consider the last time Jeffrey ate any of the stale bread. Don't be so quick to scold him. He hasn't been taking much from us for the past few weeks, we can afford to give him some bread. I'm giving him some of the apple, too."

Sophia was smiling a little, secretly. Gabriel was flushed from my unexpected reaction, and was holding his tongue. He was not thrilled about the apple, to be sure, but he wouldn't argue that with me.

"Here, Gabriel, hand the bread here. I want some. We haven't eaten since yesterday, and I'm starving from work. I'm heading back out soon to get more for the day, and I want to eat before I leave."

Gabriel, knowing that I could ask for the bread, as I was the one who worked for it and brought it home, handed it to me. I ripped off a portion and smelled it. It smelled fresh, and slightly yeasty. It did not have the musk of old water and mold, and it did not crumble away at the edges when I broke it. Already, after only one day on the job, our quality of life had improved. Continuing the O treatment was imperative

After I broke a piece of bread around where Jeffrey had bitten, I passed it to Gabriel who broke off a modest piece for both himself and for Sophia. I remembered her jam.

"Oh, Sophia, wait." I pulled out the small jar, turning it over to face her.

"This is yours. You can have it all, I remembered that you wanted some."

Gabriel would be upset that I had given the whole jar to her. Of course, she would share with everyone, but it was the idea that bothered him. I knew it was appreciated though, and that was important. I needed to keep her as an ally in this endeavor; I also genuinely wanted to thank her for keeping the Annex in order while I was taking O. And for keeping Gabriel in order.

She took the glass jar, smiling at me fully (usually, she was more reserved; full smiles opened her harelip further, and she avoided that at all costs; I appreciated her candor.) Her small hands fumbled with the lid, but opened it with a seal breaking pop. She smelled it slowly, smiling again and covering her harelip with her lower lip so that saliva would not drip out into it.

"Are you sure I can have some of this?"

Sophia, Sophia.

I didn't answer. Instead, I grabbed the bread from her hands and scooped it into the jam, bringing up a comparatively large blog. The glistening ruby blob shook slightly. Seeds poked out, giving it texture.

She looked at the chunk of bread and jam, and carefully ate it. Slowly, so that she could savor the flavors, as if even she was afraid that we couldn't sustain this type of lifestyle.

She offered a bite to Gabriel, whose face lit up in ecstasy when it hit his tongue. Both lovers sat there quietly savoring the bread and jam, and I turned away. Somehow, this was a private moment for them, and somehow I knew that this was more intimate and true than they had been in several months.

I left them in the bedroom with the bread and jam and ate my piece as I walked to the kitchen.

Jeffrey was, sure enough, digging away at the wall when I came in. When he heard me though, he stopped and came over to me.

"Knox," the words came out slowly and carefully, as if he was trying to draw them out without eliciting buzzing, "thaaaank you." It was a stutter, of sorts.

To say that I was elated would be a gross understatement. His appreciation was more important to me, more touching, than Sophia's and Gabriel's combined. I pulled out the apple from the bag in my coat pocket and held it out to him.

"Hey buddy, I have this for you too. Try it."

He took it from me more carefully than he had the bread. My heart ached for him; he didn't want to be scolded again for snatching the food, he was probably still ashamed of his snatching hands.

"Go on, you can have all of it. I just want a bite."

He handed it back to me. An offering.

I took a bite; it tasted red. It tasted cold. It tasted fruity; it tasted like the sky. After not having anything but bread for years and years, a bite of fruit is more amazing than one can imagine.

"You'll like this. I promise."

I didn't know if he had ever had an apple before. I realized that I didn't know much at all about Jeffrey prior to when he came to the mill.

Jeffrey took the apple from my extended hand, and brought it slowly to his mouth. He took a bite, stopped, then held the apple tight to his chest. He looked up at me, directly in the eyes.

"Thaaank you-uu…s' good-d."

After not eating anything but plaster for weeks and weeks, a bite of fruit is more amazing than one can imagine.

Jeffrey turned back to the wall and began picking away with one hand— the other was still holding the apple close.

~~~

I walked out of the Annex and into the mill stairway. I made my way towards the hidden entrance, always cautious, always listening and watching for Eyes and Ears.

As I lifted the board to get to the exit, I saw a Crawler peering around the corner. It was daylight, and I was heading out of the hidden entrance. I would be interested, too.

~~~

Today the streets were buzzing with people and news.

Today, the streets were Jeffrey.

"Blah blah blah, blah blah Blah blah nuclear blah blah?"

"Blah blah blah, blah war blah blah Brain blah blah."

"Imminent?"

"Blah blah blah, yes."

Today, there were less mothers and children on the street. Every man and woman today were in suits, stiff, black, grey, white. There would be no children buying yellow umbrellas today. There would be no children at all today. The telescreens were stuck on their loop.

> Do not forget your copy of the Code Of Law when leaving your house in the morning.

Please operate with regard to standard law.

Thank your Officers for their duty; report all suspected Abnormals to your districts Office.

Curfew tonight is set for 22:00.

Do not forget: Taxes are due next quarter!

I was thankful that the streets were not like this when I went out for the first time yesterday. It must have been a Dis-Work day. I was out of the mainstream for so long, I had lost track of the days of the week. That would make yesterday the only Dis-Work for the next seven days. That would mean that I might be completely dangerous and in chains by the time the next Dis-Work rolled around.

Today was Work day one, then.

And work I would.

~~~

I got straight to work cleaning windows. Today, I looked inside while I was cleaning.

The yellow umbrellas caught my eye first. I considered buying one, the impulse was almost unavoidable. I couldn't justify that, though. Maybe later in the month. Or later in the year, if I made it that long.

Next to the umbrellas was a roll of trash bags, then telescreens, then doorknobs, then cleaning supplies. A very general store.

Buzzing of the streets kept digging into my ears. Word on the street was that the Brain was currently in disaccord with another nation. Threats were being tossed around, but that

happened several times every year.
Empty threats.

> "Blah blah blah, blah blah Blah
> blah nuclear blah blah?"
> "Blah blah blah, blah war blah blah
> Brain blah blah."
> "Imminent?"
> "Blah blah blah, yes."
> *Buffalo buffalo buffalo buffalo*
> *buffalo Buffalo buffalo buffalo.*

~~~

I made four dollars. I kept it all today; Gabriel wouldn't have any reason to worry about bread servings. Even without any more work, four dollars would buy months and months of stale bread from the list. We were becoming spoiled with the good bread and jams, but we could easily go back to the old bread, if we had to.

When I got back to the Annex, Gabriel and Sophia were sleeping.

Jeffrey was curled up in the corner of the kitchen, holding the red apple tight to his chest.

And there were still only two bites taken out of it.

~*~

I was pulled immediately back onto the ship.

"Captain, my Captain!" The crewmates were desperately scattering about the deck of the boat.

"The sail is down!"

"Untie the cheese!"

"Grab the livestock!"

"Fill the balloons!"

"Captain, dear sir Captain MOVE!" I jump. A massive hand, ten thousand times too large for the wrist it was attached to, pushed me to the side with a sweaty palm. The other hand, appropriately sized, held three short strings attached haphazardly around three bulls.

"The Sails! The Sails!"

"Fill the balloons and make the sails!"

A ginger crewmate with giant blue eyes stretched one eye even larger and pressed it against my face. I fit into the pupil.

"Well, Captain, 'Fill the balloons and make the sails!'"

He passed me a curved knife with a handle of human bone. Then he left.

Three bovine stood across from me. Each one blinked their long eyelashes slowly, and one opened its mouth in a gaping yawn that swallowed half of the air around me. The eyes were apathetic. None of them started at the sight of the knife.

"Hey, someone, crew, anyone!" No one stopped to answer me.

"Hey! Crew! What is this knife! What are these cows!"

I am invisible, I'm sure.

"Well," a deep dopy sound from the direction of the cows.

"Weelll…"

I turn to the cows with the sleepy lashes and sleepy yawns and speak.

"Well, what? What do I do with this knife? How do I fill the balloon and make the sails?"

The lazy cow opened its big sleepy mouth.

"Oh Captain, my captain, you stick me in the side. Stick me in the side and fill the balloon with my yawns! Fill the balloons and make the sails! Fill the balloons and make the sails!"

The lazy cow turned to me and faced me with its big blue eye. Slowly, it bubbled outward, stretching and growing until it out grew the socket. The big eye lobbed over the side of the bovine's face and plopped onto the deck. It bounced up and into my hand, severing itself from the optical nerve that held it to the cow. It deflated.

The big cow yawned, staring at me now with two deep bloody sockets. Quickly and without thought I held the balloon up to the big cow's lazy mouth and waited for him to exhale. He did, and the deflated eyeball refilled to twice its size and began floating upward.

"Catch it Captain, catch it!" He spoke to me, his empty eyes dripping blood.

I jumped and flailed wildly but couldn't reach the floating eye.

"Hey! You! Big guy, over here! Get this!"

A string bean stalked over to the balloon and snatched it between his two hands. He carried it over to a loop of netting and placed it under. The balloon lifted again, and pulled against the net.

"I'm goin'ta yawn again soon, Captain, get the other one ready."

I obliged, and filled the balloon exactly as before, only this time, I held the balloon steady. Filled, I couldn't fit it between my outstretched hands, and had to dig my finger tips in slightly to keep a good hold on it. I brought it over to the nets, and stuffed it under a flaccid loop. It lifted and pulled tight, floating steadily next to the first eyeball.

"Now me, Captain! Now do me!" Another cow spoke to me, and bulged his eyes out.

I continued filling the balloons in this manner (except for one, one of them overfilled and popped) until all of the cows were sporting empty sockets and until all (but one) of the net loops were filled.

"Make the sails! Make the sails! Stick me and make the sails!" The first cow was singing again.

I brought the human bone knife up to his side and slid it along the length of the cow.

"Tie it all together, Captain! Tie us all together!"

The skin fell off of the cow and lay a slimy patch on the deck. The glistening blob sat wiggling and writhing against the wood. Without thinking, without seeing, I slid the knife across the other cows. One by one, the skins fell to the deck, all wiggling and bumping together. With the knife, I cut small strips along the outward facing sides of all the skins, and proceeded to tie all of those strings of flesh together. All together, the skins of the three cows formed a large, crude canvas of hair and still-raw meat. The skins stopped writhing about, and lay flat on the deck.

Before me now stood three naked cows. Three cows skinned, with muscle and tendon exposed and quivering. Each one stared at me with hollow eyes, and the sight of them repulsed me. Each cow reeked of death and decay, yet all stood, living, breathing, and chewing cud. The bottom gizzards of one of the cows heaved, and a stomach sac gurgled violently. A matted clump of debris and half digested fiber rolled up the cows exposed throat, defying the laws of gravity completely. The dripping cud sat in the mouth momentarily before the skinless bovine began chewing and grinding the mass between its flat teeth. Without skin to form a mouth (and subsequently, a food catch), masses of the vomit splattered to the wooden deck like tiny mushroom clouds. By the time the bovine re swallowed, the deck was coated in a layer of cud. The cows will starve this way, I realized.

I had to turn away from the dying cows. I lifted the skins from the deck and walked towards the giant helium filled eyeballs that danced and bounced around twenty feet above the deck. As I neared the mast, a massive blue iris rotated towards me (by no choice of its own, mind you; this was a severed eye, capable of doing only what the wind directed it to do) and pulled against the netting, impressing a grid across the giant pupil. The sight was unsettling, so I turned away. The skins still lay at my feet, so I lifted them skyward (although any direction, be it lowered or to the side would have been 'skyward' as we were sailing several thousand feet in the clouds) and affixed the quilted canvas to the various hooks and chains on the mast. At once, the skins billowed outward and pulled tight against the wind.

The crewmates gathered around me and lifted me high above their shoulders.

"Captain! Captain! Captain fixed the sails! Captain makes us go!"

From my birds eye view, I noted several of the crewmates:

One, the large fellow with the humpback that had previously (I assume) been captain seemed to have grown in size. His humpback was now debilitating, it seemed, as he was hunched almost completely over onto the deck, walking with a slow shuffle step that would soon turn to a primitive knuckle walk. His face was still extremely swollen, and the small seam where I had assumed eyes to be earlier were pinched even closer together (in elation, I suppose, due to the overwhelming and pervasive mood following the rising of the balloon and lifting of the sail.)

Another, the ginger man that, looked to the sky with his oversized blue eyes, and I wondered for a moment if he was kin to the cows, or if they were kin to him, or if he was in anyway related to the massive blue eyes of the same shade that lifted our boat high above the clouds. His eyes were dry, though, and he did not show any preference to the balloon side of the boat (as I would have expected from him had he been kin to the eyes in some way), so that was a passing notion that I almost immediately dismissed. (Incidentally, I would rethink it several minutes later, but quickly arrive at the same conclusion and drop the subject again, this time making a mental note of both my query and analysis so that I would not have to waste any further time on the trivial matters of crew-mate-and-cow-eye relations.)

The string bean crewmate stood several heads above the rest of the crew, and had to mind his head so that it wouldn't bump into me as I was being jostled about above the crewmates. Every time I would involuntarily approach the string bean in the passing pit, he would duck down low or bend his knees so that either his hands or back supported my weight. As he rose from a kneeling position on my third pass, I noticed the severity of his height. He appeared all-over tall, as if he had been placed in a taffy pull and was kneaded and pulled until all of his body parts were equally and proportionally stretched to the extreme. He was not simply tall; he was an average sized man that had his limbs and torso pulled so that the same amount of matter that once formed an average sized man now filled a man double the size.

As I was being jostled about over their heads, eerie and obscure songs began rising around me. Each crewmate sang his own tune with none competing for volume or dominance so that their individual jingles melded together to form boat wide, disjointed anthem.

"Early to club saucepans, early to crop wood-chips, makes a man Babylonian, brightly-coloured and Welsh." "I'm a telephone and I'm okay - I apply ointment to Clangers all night and I hope for road signs all day." "Party hats - pick them or love the smell of them, you can't get the ice off of windscreens with them!" "I'm a level 5 Rice cake, in spirograph-world! I've got a magic broadsword and everything!' "Do not leave, it is not favorable!" "Your mother was a suitcase and your father smelled of tea-strainers… I've never been a salamander!"

Their victory cries eventually subsided, and I was lowered to the deck again. During the festivities, the cows had expired, and all three lay stiff and dry against the deck, covered on their bottoms and bellies with half digested and stinking cud. The ginger with the large blue eye spotted this and cried out.

"Get the feast! Man the cheese wheel! Grab the champagne but do not try to fool it!"

A group of the more common crewmates scurried off with String Bean in tow. There was a great commotion and jostling, then a crash and a dull thud. I craned my neck over towards the back of the ship where the crewmates stood huddled. They tried to remain covered by the wooden captain's quarters, but were immediately visible for several reasons. First, String Bean's large stature stood out even though he was bent at a ninety-degree angle so that his torso and head were parallel to the deck and poking into the group huddle. Second, a large wheel of cheese upward of fifty feet was laying on its side, elevated several inches by a human foot and a few fingers poking out from under it. The boat shifted slightly in the wind and the wheel slipped along the deck just enough to reveal a mess of hair and another leg pinned under the massive round of cheese. One of the huddled crewmates looked up just long enough to see my observation and quickly turned back to the other still huddled crewmates. There was a panicked hush from the group, then the huddle broke and the body of the unfortunate and now crushed crewmate was dragged out from under the wheel and thrown over board quickly. The cheese wheel immediately fell back into the position physics dictated it to assume, and I was sure that if I peeked over the side of the boat I would see the body of the expired crew mate still falling through the layers of cloud.

The group of crewmates by the cheese resumed their cheerful demeanor and hoisted the cheese back up to a rolling position, then proceeded to roll it to the center of the ship (directly in front of my captain's quarters) and let it fall to its side (there was a certain caution taken this time around, and no one stood near the wheels projected landing point.) The crewmates that had been by my side resumed cheering and hooting and hollering and whooping and ran towards the giant wheel. They parted for me, and waited for me to approach the cheese before diving in with swords and gnashing teeth. The crewmates ate through the wax and dirt to get to the cheese; they didn't discriminate based upon edibility.

When the cheese was sufficiently consumed, the crewmates lifted the dry and crumbling cow corpses and broke then into hand sized portions. I was handed a portion dripping with cud and watched expectantly by the men. Not wanting to consume the mass of dry and acrid muscle, but not wanting to face alienation by the men, I took a bite, grimaced, and swallowed. Each crewmate in turn did the same, copying my hesitation and facial movements. I wondered if they would have done the same regardless of my reaction, or if they were specifically mimicking me. For the next bite, I tried to put on a look of delight, and sure enough, the crewmates did the same.

I did not like this. I was suddenly deathly afraid and wanted nothing more than to jump off the side of the ship to fall alongside the cheese crushed man.

To my absolute disbelief and horror, one of the crewmates began his jingle again, singing:

"Do not leave, it is not favorable!"
"Do not leave, it is not favorable!"
"Do not leave, it is not favorable!"

Several of the others, oblivious to reason, and following only pack mentality began singing along with the choral leader.

"Do not leave, it is not favorable!"
"Do not leave, it is not favorable!"
"Do not leave, it is not favorable!"
I held up a hand to silence them.
"Where are we headed?"
And I awoke.

Day Four

By now, I had deduced that Oxymorphin is extremely soporific. Every night, I am out as my head hits the pillow. Oddly, once I am up, I'm fully awake.

I am in the kitchen with my mother. She is wearing a pink structured dress with a lacy print. Her hair is pulled back neatly; it's not done up with curlers and sprays because we are just inside today. Just the two of us, locked in by the weather. It is raining, hard. For a moment, I am afraid that the little drops are made of glass, and that those balls of glass are going to somehow be heavier or tougher than our windows, and break right through. Now, even if that did happen, I imagine, it wouldn't be all bad. There would be broken glass everywhere, yes, and it would be a pain to clean up and fix, but no one would be seriously hurt, unless one of us fell into the glass shards from the broken window. That would be bad, but I can't see that happening. I'm too agile, and mother is wearing a pretty pink dress. She can't stumble and fall over shards of skin ripping glass in such a pretty dress, I decide. Since my mom cant get hurt, nothing can really go wrong, and I can relax about the glass rain. (The image is still stuck in my head though, and what an awful mess those shards of broken window and beads of rain make.)

Mother turns around with a spatula in one hand and a plate of pancakes in another. She is smiling, and her perfect white teeth are gleaming.

Knox, my little Knox, here, I made you breakfast. *She places the pancake plate in front of me, turns back to the stove, fills another plate with pancakes, and places that plate down next to mine. She slips into the seat next to me and hands me the entire bottle of sweet, sweet syrup.*

Go on, Knox, use as much as you want. *I inundate my island of pancakes with a syrupy sea. My mother does the same, laughing like a bell and smiling from her heart. She sticks her fork into the island and scoops up a bite; I do the same. We both eat the drippy pancake at the same time, and she looks at me and laughs a bright laugh.*

Her hand finds my hair and roughs it up.

The rain will stop soon, then we can go out and play in the yard. *She smiles sweetly; but always the yard, always the yard— why can't I go play in the street with the other kids? Why can't I play out in the park?*

I have a craving for syrup now. Years of deprivation have quelled my cravings, but with the bite of apple yesterday, many of them have returned. I resolve to buy pancake syrup for myself today. I'll hide it in my coat pocket so that I can keep it to myself. I'm not greedy, but all of the other roommates have their own special things. Gabriel has Sophia, Sophia has her jam, and Jeffrey has his apple. I, on the other hand, have nothing. (I realize now, after saying that, that that is a lie.

I have perhaps the greatest special thing of all; I have the ability to go out in the normal world; to see the sky and sunsets, to smell the dirt and feel it under my shoes; to walk around in the normal world; to just simply leave the mill. So I apologize for lying just then.)

This morning, as I get out of the mattress, I am alone in the room. Gabriel and Sophia are not waiting around for me to wake up and show them what I've purchased for them, and I am thankful.

Instead, Gabriel is seated in the main room with his Sophia wrapped around him. She arms are hung loosely over his shoulders and she is holding a piece of bread with a coating of sticky red paste. Gabriel is holding a piece of the bread too, but his is unadorned.

Both look up and smile as I enter the room.

"Off to work, Mr. Normal?" Gabriel says.

Sophia laughs at the 'Mr. Normal' bit. Clearly, they are both in a bright mood today.

And Jeffrey, as usual, is in the kitchen picking away at the holes in the wall. Today, though, he is only using one hand. The other is holding the apple, still missing only two bites. The red skin is still vibrant, but the edges around the bites are puckering slightly, and the once white and juicy meat has browned and dried up.

With everyone content in the Annex, I left through the rusted doors and headed for the stairs. After only three days of walking around with the Normals, I had grown quite accustomed to higher standards of living; in the years prior, the bands of light and dust in the maze of the hallways were a non-issue. Now, though, they bothered me more than they should, and I found myself anxious to get back outside.

I made it to the first floor and towards the hidden exit panel when I heard a scuffling from behind me. I turned. It was the Crawler again, same from yesterday. He lingered a little longer this time. It was unnerving; the Crawlers had always ignored us when we walked through the hallways, and now one was watching me several days in a row. Granted, I *was* leaving through the hidden entrance only a few days after calling a meeting to tell the other mill tenants to stay indoors (I can see now how that might have made me look like a giant fibber or a complete asshole.) I took a step towards the Crawler to scare him off, but instead of slinking back into his room as they normally would, he took a step closer to me.

"Hello." His voice was a cheese grater and snaked its way along the walls and around my head. I granted him the courtesy of a response.

"Yes?"

He became shifty, not having expected a response from one of the Annex tenants.

"Well, see, me and my people, well we've been seeing ya leaving the mill for a few days now...we were under the impression that we couldn't do that. That the eyes were watching us and the borders. So say, tell me you haven't been playing a war, have you? Not trying to block us in without food or supplies, eh?"

He was a type of nervous animal, and his words came out quickly and forced.

"No, no, not at all. We were serious about the Eye officer, and I can tell you for sure that there are many of them out and about lately. Yes, I've been outside the mill. But I'm not at risk. You see," I paused, wondering if I should share more information, "you see, I have started taking O."

His slacked jaw sealed up quickly. I could see his heart rate elevating with his breathing, and it drummed out in the echoing hallway.

"O-ox-oxymorphin, you say?"

I nodded.

"Oh."

Exactly.

"Yes. Oh."

He was silent.

"It's.. it has been working, for now. I've been able to get a job outside of the mill and.." I didn't want to share too much information with him. After all, I couldn't afford to bring back supplies for all of the other mill tenants too.

He also didn't know about Jeffrey, and I decided to stop before I indulged him that. If he for any reason thought I was a danger, he could have the Crawlers take me out right here, and the Annex mates might not even know that anything was awry until tomorrow morning. By then, I could be dead. So I closed my mouth.

"Oh. Well, then. We've had an encounter with O, in our space. And some of our guys were lost. So, just, well I didn't say this, but just watch ya self, okay?"

He was worried about me, and I was shocked.

"Yeah, we've had an encounter too."

He had put it out there first. I felt that we had broken the boundaries of rivalry, if only temporarily.

"Well, luck with that. Ha, ha, if ya ever got some extra scrap, you can send it our way."

A friendship offering. A joke, of sorts. He didn't think that I would, but maybe now I'd pick something up for him, or at least give him a piece of something. Maybe some of my syrup later. Maybe.

~~~

It was raining outside; glass droplets that fell hard and fast and shattered on the pavement below me.

Apparently, in the rain, window cleaning services are not required. I showed up to work anyway, though, and the clerk put me to work. He had me dusting shelves and reordering Official sponsored supplies. Up close I noticed the Official seal on all of the stores items; a gold circular stamp containing the phrase 'oboedire auctoritas'. Funny that an Official managed store would hire an Abnormal on O.

The shelves were coated in a thick layer of dust in some areas of the store; often, these were un-stocked areas or areas with obscure items. The clerk was weary of me for a while, keeping his eyes on me as I made my way to the far corners of the store. Of course, I wouldn't be stealing anything from the store. That would be far, far too risky, and I couldn't even contemplate being captured by the Officials.

~~~

There are several theories about just what happens when an Abnormal is caught.

Some optimistics say that we are only sentenced to a lifetime in a segregated jail. A few of the rogues that have wandered through the mill over the years have said that they know a guy, that knows a guy, that knows a guy that was captured and put in jail. Still gets letters, they say, and sometimes he plans an escape. Sometimes.

Descriptions of the jail cells themselves have varied from each retelling; once we heard that the cells were just like Normal cells, only for 'Abnormals Only' and had thicker bars and glass paneling for the Abnormals that could cut through metal or slip through spaces or something similar. Another common description details small rooms with solid concrete walls, four feet thick in all directions, and no air vents. (This, in my opinion, sounds a little bit more like what might actually exist, if the jail theory is true, that is.)

There are also a few oddities, such as a giant open room with Abnormals hanging from meat hooks, in a sort of Abnormal meat locker (minus the refrigeration).

But to be honest, I'm not so sure we'd be granted the privilege of a jail sentence.

A more plausible theory suggests that we are simply killed. On the spot, in a different location, the details vary, but this is the most commonly held belief. This would, of course, make the most sense. Why deal with us, when all the Officials want is to make us disappear? It would be so very easy for both effort and cost purposes to capture the Abnormals, line them up in rows or take them solitary, and shoot them down. Or knife the shit out of one of the helpless ones, if you're a real sadistic Official. It is also believed that our bodies are used to make glue. No need for horses in this day and age, try Abnormal Glue!

Slavery is another common and plausible theory. A few of the rogues have claimed to have escaped slavery and run away to the mill and other safe houses. Sometimes, I'm not so sure this would be too much better than being immediately killed. (Or even slowly tortured and killed.) I'm not so sure that I could want to live in the captivity and bondage of the same people that rejected us and forced us into hiding. How ironic would that be; and entire puppet government ruled by a handful of Normals and run by millions of the very race they discriminate against.

Then, of course, there are a few eccentrics that have fanciful delusions about the fate of the captured. We are captured then treated like kings! Worshipped by the Official as gods and mighty angels! Questioned as the

Oracle for the Brain! They need us, they say, they are not looking for us in order to eliminate us, no, no friends, they are looking for us because they are enthralled with us, crave our presence, need our wisdom! These are the Abnormals that run out into the streets in the middle of the day to surrender to an Eye or an Ear. These are the Abnormals that are most likely killed. These are the Abnormals that work the telescreens that remind the Normals of their Normal duties and of their superior Official Government.

Natural selection in action, I guess.

~~~

The clerk closed the store early because of the rain and the lack of customers. As he walked to the register to get my pay for the day's work (four thirty four, to be exact) I noticed for the first time just how much younger than me this clerk was.

He must have been nineteen or twenty, and I was well into my thirties (at least, I think so). He wasn't particularly attractive either. He had a round face and close set eyes, with ears that were just a little too big and a nose that was just a little crooked. He had a few acne scars on his face, and his skin was several shades of pink.

Had any of these features been just a little more obvious, he would be one of us, one of the Abnormals. It was pure luck that he was *just* normal enough to pass as safe.

I thought of Sophia; without her harelip, she would be a Normal, for sure. And a beautiful one, at that. She would be famous; an actress, or a face of the government. She would be rich, and would be with a normal Gabriel—a trophy wife that never had to hide in a broken down mill, a trophy wife that could have as many apples and jams as she wanted.

This broke my heart, a little.

On the way back to the mill, I stopped into the market and picked up a bottle of syrup for myself.

I knew that I'd be making a stop to the Crawler's mill space.

I wasn't yet sure if I was going to share the syrup with my Annex family. I needed something just for me. This syrup was just for me.

~~~

The rain was still coming down hard as I turned the corner to get back to the mill. The buildings were ending, and the city's foot traffic almost completely stopped at this corner. The shattering raindrops were more obvious here, and I worried that my shoes wouldn't be thick enough to protect my feet from the broken glass.

~~~

Standing at the corner of the mill lot was a suit with a mirrored mask. A fabric eye stared at me, seeing through the suit I wore and the drugs I took.

I slowed to a stop, looked around like I was lost, then walked along the side of the mill lot, hoping he wouldn't come over to the lone pedestrian for questioning. I didn't hear him behind me, but the shattering glass was loud enough to cover just about any human noise. There was a flash of black to my right, along the far edge of the mill opposite the Eye. I turned; it was a swinging door, or at least a swinging board.

Interesting. I hadn't ever seen this entrance before. A hand followed the opening of the door, and a familiar figure emerged into the shadow.

Z— not quite Normal, but not quite Abnormal, either.

He hurried me inside and closed the panel behind me. He picked two long rods off the ground and stuck them through holes that ran through the panel and into the brick, securing the panel in place and blending the seam. A seamless entrance that put our secret entrance to shame. But that was to be expected of Z.

"He's been out there all day."

In his way, he said everything and nothing all at once.

"Thank you." I needn't say more, he wouldn't like too much more, anyway.

"Come, follow me back upstairs Knox, we have a discussion that's been looming for a while now."

Z had not talked to me this way since the others began moving into the mill. For a while, he kept me sheltered in the third floor, in the room I stay in now. Occasionally, he would come down to talk to me, keep me company. I was a small child at that point, and he was a father figure. He might have been ten years older than me, but a million years wiser to the world of Abnormality.

I followed him up a staircase that I had never seen. This one, unlike ours and unlike any of the others in the mill, was almost perfectly preserved.

Small areas were patched up with wooden boards or discolored plaster, but the majority was solid and original.

I wondered what his living space looked like, with stairs like these.

The stairs went on forever, and we must have walked all the way into the cosmos. We hit the summit, and at the top was a solid metal door; no rust, no dents, no holes. He had an actual doorknob, and two locks (one pad lock and a standard door knob lock.) He opened them all from a bundle of keys in his pocket, and motioned for me to step inside.

Z's space was far beyond what I could have imagined. He had a large space, possibly the entire top floor, with sectioned rooms that fully closed and had their own doors, some locking, some not. Farthest from where we were standing was a full bed; metal frame, blanket, and full mattress. On the side of the bed was a shelving unit that had rows and rows of hand bound and commercial bound notebooks.

Directly in front of us was an old couch. He sat down, and motioned for me to do the same.

"You are on Oxymorphin now, Knox."

A statement. I didn't know if he wanted me to confirm this or wait for him to continue. I settled between the two and nodded.

"That is dangerous, as I am sure you already know."

I realized that he must have been referring to Jeffrey's incident, but how he knew about this, I did not know.

"I too have thought about and seriously considered taking Oxymorphin, at times. But it has always been just thoughts, Knox. I do not have the luxury of roommates that you do. It would be far too dangerous for me to take O."

I wasn't sure what he was getting at, or even if he was getting at anything. Maybe he was just talking, or maybe he had something important to tell me. I wasn't sure.

"In any case, I don't disapprove of you taking Oxymorphin. I would caution you to be careful, and stop taking it if you notice signs of lunacy, but until then, I admire your courage. I do have to ask you to be very, very careful though.

"I've noticed that you have been using the "hidden" escape. That will not do. There have been more and more Eyes venturing towards the edge of the city, like you've seen today. They will start to notice you. And for everyone else's sake, you need to be more careful from now on. Leave while it is still dark, and scope out the area from the cracks on the first and second floors before you leave in the mornings."

Of course I would do that. After today's encounter with the Eyes, he didn't have to tell me to watch out.

We were silent. I'm sure that he, like I, was remembering our past of companionship. It had been several years since we stayed together, and the time was felt heavily now.

"So, Z, how long have you…" I looked around the large and organized mill space, "how long have you been…here?"

Z chuckled a little and looked around too.

"I've been here all along, Knox, my old friend. Spent quite a bit of time up here, can you tell?"

His eyes were smiling, and I laughed a little. Clearly, he spent massive amounts of time organizing and setting up the space.

Aside from individual rooms with locked doors, there was a large kitchen space with an old stove and a sink. There were several large tables in the area, and a few closely but not perfectly matched chairs. He had a track lighting of sorts set up, but without modern lights. Gas lamps were hung from metal wires that were stung across the stove and sink area. Near the kitchen was a large open cupboard (not open by choice, there were no doors equipped on the shelves) stocked full of breads, cans of preserved food, jars of jellied foods, dried fruits, and dried meats. Meats. I hadn't eaten meat since I left my mother's home. It was far too expensive on the list service, and the portions given were small, not nearly large enough to feed an entire room of people. Most meats were not dried properly, either, and would end up rotting visibly, or worse, rotting slowly from the remaining blood and juices within the seemingly dried meat. The area we were in had, as I previously mentioned, a case of journal-like books, a small end table, a larger table with papers and pens sprawled across the top, a large couch that we currently sat on, and two cushioned one seated chairs. Comfortable, to be sure, and classier than anything else in the mill.

The walls were in great shape, too.

Unlike the walls of the lower floors, these were plastered over where cracks had formed, and all of the doors were solid and without holes or rust.

Anyone else would have assumed that Z was rich (for an Abnormal) or would have no other clue as to how he obtained all of his amenities. I knew, however, from previous discussions, that he had acquired most, if not all, of his furnishings from old storage rooms in the mill. Prior to the reclaiming of the mill by Abnormals, it had been used as a storage space for Normals and Abnormals (undercover, of course) that could afford the monthly rent. At some point, the renters abandoned their storage spaces, and many simply left their unused and unwanted junk in the rooms. As they say, one man's trash is another man's treasure....

Anyway, Z came along and stumbled across these rooms upon rooms of stuff. Endless space, it seemed, and all the furnishings anyone could ever want or need. He found the top rooms, the most preserved, for whatever reason, and he claimed it as his. Over the next few months, he would drag furnishings up the stairways to the top space, knocking down walls and building new ones where he saw fit. By the time I arrived, there were only several useful items left in the old storage spaces, and Z gave me my run of them. I took mattresses, a refrigerator, tables, and a couch. Everything else was complete junk, or furniture in such disrepair that it would have been more trouble than it was worth. I assume that as the other tenants have moved in, they have rummaged through the spaces. Perhaps they have taken some of the furnishings, perhaps not. I had not been inside any of the other tenants' rooms, since they had moved in, that is. They could all be unfurnished completely for all I knew.

Sometimes, we still look through the storage spaces, hoping for any treasure that had been buried or overlooked. More often than not, we do not find anything, but bits of wall and other debris can be useful in repairs and other building endeavors.

So in short, it did not surprise me that Z had such elaborate furnishings in his mill space. I only wished I could have looked around and behind the locked doors. I'd imagine that there would be beds, and couches, and tables, and perhaps even some old art or televisions. I could only imagine so much, though, and knew that there had to be more behind some of the doors.

I also noticed that Z was wearing different clothing than I was accustomed to seeing him in. He must also have large supplies of clothing, I realized stupidly. I looked down at my worn fraying and faded suit and felt slightly self-conscious. He would understand though, undoubtedly.

I looked back to Z after having looked around his apartment from sometime, to notice him watching me. I wondered what he had brought me here for. He had already saved me for the day, and had shown me a new secret entrance. I did not know, however, why he had brought me up to his space. Maybe he felt that I should see it, after knowing him for so long and for never seeing anything above the third floor. Maybe he wanted to show it off to a lesser tenant. Maybe he was lonely up here year after year by himself, and wanted the company of an old companion. Or maybe he just wanted to warn a potential danger to both himself and the other tenants of the risks involved with trying to merge with the Normal world.

Perhaps it was a bit of all of those.

His voice crackled over the silence.

"You are welcome here anytime, you know. Just you, though. I hope you will understand. I do not mid the presence of your roommates, but I would not want to share my space with them."

He walked over and placed a warm, rough hand on my shoulder.

"But for you, old friend, if you ever need a place to go for the night, or need a more experienced supervisor as you progress with your O experiment, please, I ask you to find me."

"Just get into the entrance I showed you today. I have cameras linked to the stairwell, all entrances, and all hallways. I will see you, and let you in."

Cameras in all the hallways and entrances. I was not sure that this was alright. He must have read my face, because he looked sheepish suddenly and dropped his gaze to the side towards one of the closed and locked rooms.

"It's a safety measure, really. It's important for me to know who is where in the building if I need to know. You forget, I am in charge of protecting the mill, basically, and *I too* am in danger if something goes wrong."

I could understand that.

I wondered how long my old friend had watched me and the other tenants

on cameras and monitors. If he spend
all day at the screens, or if he only
stopped by briefly to check up on
people and safety. I wasn't sure what I
would do, if I had been in his situation.

Loneliness could drive a man to
near anything.

He still looked sheepish, and spoke
quickly to me now.

"Knox, let me show you."

He got up from the couch and
walked towards one of the far rooms. I
got up and followed him, and he paused
outside of the door, perhaps wondering
if he should show me. I was careful to
not show hesitation; I wanted more than
anything to see what he could see.
Needed to, all of a sudden. The urge
was overwhelming.

Z opened the door to the room, and
we were immediately faced with a wall

of glowing monitors. Turning to the side, I was faced by another wall completely filled by monitors. Ten by ten, monitors displayed dark hallways and familiar corners. I could see the third floor hallway, from both ends, the stairway, all of the second floor, and first floor. I could see into the New Tenants room, could see where all of them, all five of them, were sitting, standing, moving, what all of them were doing. I felt like I was overstepping my boundaries, and should be able to see these interactions and rooms.

The Crawlers were completely exposed, too. Like I had earlier thought, the Crawler's space was completely devoid of furnishings. Instead of chairs, they had mounds of rubble that several of them were sprawled across. There were no tables, no signs of running water or food storage. True to form, they moved close to the ground, slinking around and avoiding direct contact, which was surprising to me, as I had assumed that that behavior was reserved for public outings.

And I could see into our mill space.

I wondered if Z was proud when he saw our space. It was by far superior to the other tenants', and we seemed more organized than all of the groups. We had definitive sleeping spaces, living spaces, eating spaces. I could see Jeffrey's holes. I did not like that. I did not like that this old friend could see so much and know so much about my closest friend. I felt that he should not spy on Jeffrey, of all people. But that was a passing thought.

Currently, Jeffrey was huddled in a corner, holding an object (I knew it had to be the apple; since I had given it to him, he had held on to it. It was browning fast, and would soon start to rot, but I had no doubt that he would hold onto it. It was the only token of affection, only sign that any of us even tolerated him, since the O incident. The thought of this made my heart ache, and I found myself faced with the desire to give him apples every day.) Gabriel was staring out one of the cracks, probably looking for me, and Sophia had her arms draped loosely over his shoulder, and looked just as concerned as Gabriel. Curious, I thought, as they had been asleep every night when I got home. I wondered if they spent every night this way, looking out for me and worrying. Perhaps today they just saw the Eye.

I was even surprised to see an outside view of the city street corners leading to the apartment. This would be useful, definitely, and was more likely than not how Z kept himself safe from the Eyes and how he spotted me today (I had wondered how he had noticed me and my predicament given his lack of windows and cracks.)

I knew that I couldn't stay with Z for long, if ever. We could get along fine, and we were surely the best suited to live together, as we had been here the longest and were by far the most Official cautious tenants, but I couldn't leave my roommates to fend for themselves. I could not leave Jeffrey. I could not leave Sophia. I could not even leave Gabriel, although I was sure that he would believe himself fit to lead the Annex. They needed me to keep order.

And if I left now, they would wonder if I was dead. (And it would have to come to that; I couldn't decide to live with Z and tell them; they would want to join, and wonder why they couldn't. Even if they didn't, they would always wonder what the fourth floor was like, what I was doing, what they didn't know…I wouldn't do that to them. I probably wouldn't even tell them about today's incidents.)

I looked over to Z; I had seen enough. In typical Z fashion, he immediately knew my intentions.

"Z, thank you for today. And thank you for showing me…"

I motioned to the rest of the mill space,

"this. I may end up taking you up on the offer if I need help with O later on, or if I need a place to stay for a night for whatever reason. But I can't live with you, for now anyway. It has been nice seeing you; really nice; but I cannot leave my roommates. They need me, for now. Thank you, though. I will be back."

He knew all of this already, of course. He smiled a sad, knowing smile; he knew I couldn't stay with him; he knew he wanted me to.

"I understand, my friend. Please come back, if it suits you."

I made it to the door before he spoke again.

"It gets lonely up here, Knox."

That stopped me. I turned back to him, and reached into my coat pocket.

I pulled out the syrup bottle, and handed it to him.

"Have this. I will be back. I bought this for myself; a gift. I need one. You may have as much as you would like, I just ask that you save me a spoonful. I'll be back sometime soon to share a few spoons with you."

The sadness did not leave Z's eyes or smile, but he thanked me.

I turned and walked out of the space back to the hidden entrance before I could stop and change my mind.

~*~

"The scar, the portal, Captain, we are headed to the scar!"

Frustrated with the seemingly constant nonsense streaming from the crewmates, I bowed to the crew and thanked them for the feast and festivities. Then I left for my captain's quarters.

I was finally alone.

The inside was furnished with velvet and polished wood. Immediately upon walking in, a large cushioned throne gleamed in the light from the darkened portholes. The light in the room was slightly golden from the tinting used in the glass, and everything inside took on an ethereal glow.

To the side was a large wooden table topped with an earthly globe with an intricate golden base and many large pins with brightly colored gems affixed to their tops. Several of the gem-topped pins were stuck in to the globe while others were stuck loosely into the wooden table so that they would not roll away with the movements of the boat. Across from this table was a smaller table with plain wooden chairs around it, presumably for meetings with important crewmates. One was slightly thinner in width and drastically taller in height, which suggested immediately that String Bean was one of the previous captain's favorites. I made a mental note to keep an eye on him, as he may very well be suited for me as well.

The one thing notably absent in the lavish quarters was a bed.

Odd, I thought.

But oh, that's right;

I'm only dreaming.

I woke up on my mattress pad back in the Annex. Several feet away, Sophia had herself wrapped around Gabriel, and Jeffrey was pressed up against the ceiling, buzzing like a fridge.

Day Five

I was more nervous today than I had been any other day about leaving the mill. Compared to Z's entrance, the common "hidden" entrance was completely exposed and obvious.

I didn't want to leave that way because I feared a snake might eat me up.

An Eye, rather.

~~~

The entire mill looked different having seen Z's space. What was once a comfortable living area was now a shack like and barren room – our kitchen was now little more than a playground for Jeffrey. What was different for me, though, was the same, unchanged, for everyone else. Sophia and Gabriel sat in their corner, wrapped around each other, talking quietly and only for themselves, and Jeffrey followed his typical and expected routine. (The apple, of course, was a new addition, but I had expected to see that. I might have even been a little sad if I had seen that he discarded it.) No one else had seen the other space. No one else knew how little we had.

I left the Annex. The hallway was banded with plates of light. Always there, at least during the day, but I had never seen just how solid they were.

They were full plates.

I put my hand to one of the walls of light. I couldn't see through to the other side, and knew that my hand would be stopped right.... n

What?

My hand went right through.

I closed my eyes and ran through the hallway.

Had I not lived in the mill for so long, I might have hit walls, or fallen down stairs, or impaled myself upon jagged pipes.

But I've been here for quite a while.

When I opened my eyes I found myself at the beginning of the hall leading to the hidden entrance.

The Crawler's space.

I remembered my Crawler, then realized that I had given my syrup to Z. What a stupid, stupid decision.

I resolved to bring him a small candy, instead.

I pushed aside the paneling to the outside and stepped through. The ground was glue, and I found my feet stuck. How inconvenient. I became fidgety and shifty so that the Eyes couldn't see me. They can only see you if you're standing still. They can't see movement. They can only see you if you're moving around.

There were way too many people on the street—they were suffocating me with their hot breath and buzzing earpieces.

This is the windows and clean away until job. I'd spray the cleaner on for a minute there, I lost minute there, I lost myself. But myself, I lost myself.

Phew, for I noticed that they were already much enamored buzzing fridge.

He's like a detuned radio.

Official police, the windows were completely clear. Arrest this girl her Hitler hairdo is buzzing like a fridge. Talking in maths. Official police, I've given all I can it's your Party. This is what you'll get.

This lost myself found myself at my window cleaning lost myself. This is what I walked down the streets and I lost myself, I lost myself.

Karma police, arrest this man, he is the mill. And for a minute there, I lost myself, I feel ill.

And we have crashed.

I'm dizzy with stupid thoughts. Drunk with stupid thoughts. For a minute there, I lost myself. But I'm back, and I have a pocket full of change and a candy bar to buy.

~~~

Finding the candy store was easy enough, although you'd think it would be harder in a city of stiff grey suits and fluorescent telescreens. But there it was. Grey, like every other building, but with a small LED display sign that read in the plainest of scripts: Confections.

The window was clean; someone just like me must have recently been by. That, or children had not been pressing their noses and hands against the glass as they did when I was little.

"Knox, today we're going out for a surprise!"

A surprise? Going out? But, I'm never allowed out, I remember thinking, *I'm never allowed out mother.*

"Knox, here, put on your trousers, we're heading out!"

Out. We are heading out. Outside.
Past the picket fence? Probably not. We
probably weren't going far out.

Mother came over to me with my
corduroy trousers and I stepped into
them. 'Clothes just weren't made like
this anymore,' she'd say when I was
even smaller. 'They just don't
appreciate a good material and a good
fit! All boxes! All boxy!'

I guess she has a point, I'd think.
Every man that walked by our fence
was square. His suit was grey and he
was a box. And the mothers and
children were no better. No shape, no
shape, no color. My mother always
wore shape and color. She was an
antique woman. That's what she'd often
say. "I'm an antique woman, a fifties
gal."

I didn't know what a gal was.

Mother pulled the shades and turned on a light in the house. Made it look like we were inside when we were really outside. I never knew why she did this.

"Come on, Knox, come over here! I have a surprise for you!"

I followed her out the door. Our grass was green and bright and full of little springs. It crunched down a little under our feet as we walked.

Mother stopped at the white fence and stared around the corner for a moment. She turned back to me, beaming brightly in her fifties gal dress, and opened the fence.

Outside, outside. Why was she taking me out of the fence? Hadn't she always told me to never leave the fence?

"Little Knox, hold Mother's hand."

I grabbed her hand and followed her through the fence to the sidewalk immediately behind it. It seemed like we left behind a world of color and stepped into a world of grey and static and boxes and fluorescence. We did, really.

The sidewalk was solid grey, a reflection of the buildings and sky. It was perfectly leveled; there were no organic bumps or imprints made in the cement as it dried. Everything outside was geometric; the sidewalk, and the buildings, and the trees, and the shrubs, and the signs, and the people, and the briefcases held by the people. The people. After walking farther into the city, we were surrounded by people. They were all the same, mind you, all the same man, just one guy walking around in his suit and carrying his briefcase. There were thousands of him, and they all buzzed with serious business conversation.

There was another buzzing, though. This one came from a little higher up. A television. We had one in our house, but ours was rounded and had a bubbled screen, like there was a guy inside of it pushing hard against the glass trying to escape. That was nonsense, though. There was no little guy inside our television. No invisible man trying to push his way out of the glass screen, Mother told me so. But this television was different. The screen was flatter, and the color was brighter, but thousands of times plainer than ours. Our television showed guy and girls running around and dancing, wearing bright outfits and singing happy songs that Mother would sometimes hum along with. This television showed only one thing; a pair of lips, plain, slightly pink, and a little dry, definitely thin, definitely a man's lips, and these lips were speaking to us, to everyone, slowly, carefully, e- nun- ci- a- ting e- ver- rey word, so that no one could misunderstand him.

> *Do not forget your copy of the Code Of Law when leaving your house in the morning.*
> *Please operate with regard to standard law.*
> *Thank your Officers for their duty; report all suspected Abnormals to your districts Office.*
> *Curfew tonight is set for 22:00.*
> *Do not forget: Taxes are due this quarter!*

Over and over and over. He rattled on, over and over again, stopping every

now and then to lick his dry lips with a
flat pink tongue. Then it would loop
back to the beginning, and repeat.
Every building had one of these screens
affixed to it. Every street corner had
one posted slightly above people's
heads. I asked mother what they were,
they were not like the televisions I had
seen.

"Telescreens, Knox."

She didn't say anything else about
them.

We passed hundred of these
screens, all telling us the same thing
until I could close my eyes and repeat
exactly, word for word, what the man
was telling us, making my lips form the
same shapes that his did.

"Do not forget your copy of the
Code Of Law when leaving your
house in the morning.

Please operate with regard to standard law.
Thank your Officers for their duty; report all suspected Abnormals to your districts Office.
Curfew tonight is set for 22:00. Do not forget: Taxes are due next quarter!"

I got bored of walking and started copying the telescreens out loud. My eyes were closed, and I started quiet, but as I realized that there was no way that I could forget a word and mess up, I spoke up louder and spoke with more confidence. Mother jabbed me hard with her elbow and hushed me quickly. I kept my lips closed after that.

We finally stopped in front of a store— it was a little less plain than the other stores, but only because of the cardboard cutouts hanging in the window. I pressed my face against the window to see farther inside; my print matched up exactly with hundreds and hundreds of prints before it.

Immediately in front of me were rows of colorful candies; each one was a paint drop that spattered against the grey city. There were gold wrappers, and pink wrappers, and blue wrappers, and purple wrappers, and red wrappers, and green wrappers, and striped wrappers, and candies dipped in chocolate, and candies that looked like colored glass, thousands and thousands of candies that I had never even heard of, let alone seen. Mother pulled on my hand and led me inside.

None of these candies were placed in the window when I went back today. There were no cardboard cut outs, no candies on display, and no beaming children.

People today were not for candy. People today were skinny boxes.

I stepped in through the doorway. In front of me were a few plain tables, each covered with a few small boxes of candy. That was it. No displays, no rows upon rows upon rows of colorful candy. There were no blues, or pinks, or oranges, or purples, of reds, or greens, or striped candies, or gold wrappers. All of the candies in front of me were wrapped in a plain white paper, stamped with both the Official logo and the name of the candy, which was printed in plain black print.

Chocolate, small.
Chocolate, medium.
Chocolate, large.
Caramel, small.

Caramel, medium.
Caramel, large.
Toffee, small.
Toffee, medium.
Toffee, large.
Three candies. Three sizes.
Chocolate, caramel, toffee.

I wondered what mothers did today to take their kids out for a surprise. I wondered what children did.

I grabbed two large chocolates, which were not really large at all, rather close in shape and size to a golf ball, and stepped up to the clerk's post.

He watched me. I was still gripping to the floor with my toes so that it wouldn't melt away from under me.

"This all."

I wasn't sure whether or not I was supposed to answer. Had he asked me a question? I couldn't remember.

"Just these."

"That'll be 2.70."

That was all that I had made that day, plus change from the day before. There would be no money for the Annex mates if I kept buying small indulgences like this. It would stop after today. Day five. Two days left, maybe. We needed money. I handed over the cash though, regardless. My Crawler would experience a candy, if it cost me everything (I couldn't go out on Oxymorphin without giving something to someone as sheltered and hidden as the Crawler.)

The clerk watched me place the money on the counter, shifting slightly on the wooden floors.

"Hey buddy, what's your deal."

Not a question, and I was glad. I stopped gripping to the floor, and for a few moments was afraid that I would fall into it.

I grabbed the two large chocolate candies off from the counter and left the store. From a grey room to a grey city.

(On my last few steps in the candy store, my feet had become sucked into the muck of the floor and I had to pick them up hard in order to free them and move them. I gripped immediately to the cement outside. The watchful eyes of the clerk were hidden behind a wall now.)

~~~

Inside the mill, the light was no longer forming walls. It had dulled to a twilight, and the bands of light peeking through were translucent. I stepped through them with ease.

I came up to the Crawlers' space and didn't know what to do.

Should I knock?

I hoped that he would answer the door, but didn't know if he would.

I tried anyway.

Knock.

Knock.

Knock.

I heard slinking and movement from behind the door. In a few seconds, the door creaked open, just enough for a wary eye to look out. The door remained half open for a few moments, then there was some more shuffling, and my Crawler opened the door fully.

He stepped outside, slinking around the wall on the way out.

He looked at me.

I looked at him.

Neither of us had much to say.

I pulled out one of the large chocolates and split it in two. I handed it over to the scrawny man, and he held it in his hand.

He stared at it.

He had no idea what it was or what to do with it. I had been right when I figured he had never seen a candy.

"Eat it, it's a chocolate."

His eyes widened.

"A, a Chocolate?"

As if it was a revered treasure.

"Yes."

He stared at me open mouthed for a few more moments, then spoke.

"You got me, you got me a chocolate?"

"Well, half. Half of a chocolate. But it's big. So it's really kind of more like a whole small chocolate."

He looked back at the candy in his hand, and then brought it up to his nose. He smelled it, then brought it up to his lips.

I turned and left, leaving him to the chocolate.

I walked right through the walls of light. The walls that weren't walls, really, after all.

For the first time, I noticed a patch of wall slightly newer than its surroundings. The plaster was fresher, and it was not crumbling in as many places as it was in the older sections of the mill.

Z's stairway. It must have been. I tapped along the new section of the wall, and it sounded and reverberated. Hollow. A stairwell. I followed the new wall, tapping along it to find hollow spaces, running along it until it came to an end in a dark, lightless room. I felt my way along the wall, not knowing what I was looking for, but knowing that it had to be there, somewhere.

A ha.

Along the bottom of the wall, close to the rotting floor, a section of the plastered wall was broken away. A hole perfectly sized for a person. A hole perfectly sized for me. Z had made me a hole, recently, maybe, because dust and debris from the missing drywall were littered on the floor. I crawled through, and found myself in the stairwell.

Surprise, surprise.

I walked quickly and quietly up the stairs. I'm not sure why, though, because he had cameras placed throughout the stairs. I knew it. I had seen it. I knew he'd be waiting at the top of the stairs.

And he was.

"You found the hole, I see."

Z, my Z.

I was unreasonably mad.

"What were you thinking, putting that there? You had your space perfectly protected. One entrance. One exit. Why would you open up a second? Why would you open up a second so unprotected?" I was seething.

Z was chuckling, in his way.

He wrapped a hand around my back and patted my shoulders.

"Knox, Knox, Knox. No one else will find that. No one else will see the stairwell. No one else even knows what to look for. And when we stop talking again, for whatever reason, be it Jeffrey or be it the Oxymorphin, I can easily recover it. Do not worry so much, Knox, my friend."

I did not like that he thought that we would stop talking again. That he would have to recover the hole. That he knew Jeffrey's name, or that I preferred Jeffrey to the other Annex mates. I did not like that at all, but I liked Z. My old friend.

Without thinking, I pulled the other remaining half of the large chocolate out of my pocket and held it out to him.

He looked at it, like the Crawler had, but he knew exactly what it was.

He smiled, and I was elated.

"Thank you, Knox."

He ate the chocolate, holding it on his tongue and letting it dissolve. The smart way to eat a chocolate. The Crawler wouldn't know this. The Crawler would eat it all at once in excitement, and then not have any more.

I should have told him. What a waste of chocolate.

I turned and left Z just as I had done with the Crawler. I walked back down the perfect stairs and crawled back out through the hole. I looked back at it, and wanted to cover over it right then. But I didn't. I wanted to see Z again, regardless of how much he knew, regardless of how much I didn't want him to know.

~~~

By the time I got back to the Annex, it was dark outside. There were no bands of lights, no walls of bright light. I walked back with complete ease.

Gabriel and Sophia were curled up together on the floor of the living room.

Drool was seeping out from the top of her mouth, from the opening of her harelip. Her Abnormality. Gabriel was talking, cussing in his sleep, his Abnormality.

I left them in the living room and walked in to the kitchen to find Jeffrey.

He was awake, holding the apple, and sitting in a pile of debris from the cement walls. He was staring up at me, and for the first time I looked around at the wreckage of the kitchen. I was amazed, and slightly awed by Jeffrey's hard work. Large holes were dug into every wall of the kitchen, and large piles of debris were under each one. I looked back at Jeffrey; he saw that I had appreciated his work. It clearly meant a lot to him.

I handed him the last chocolate, hoping that he'd eat all of it, as he had

the bread on the first day. He didn't
though. He took a bite out of the
chocolate and handed the rest of the
chocolate ball to me.

"Thank you, Jeffrey."

He smiled and gnawed at his chunk
of candy. I sat down next to him and ate
mine too. We sat in silence for a few
minutes, or maybe a few hours, then
drifted off to sleep on the kitchen floor,
among the rubble of Jeffrey's
destruction.

~*~

I knew not to think about the bed this time.

Temptations, temptations.

I left the captain's quarters and stepped back out to the deck.

The scar, the scar.. what the hell was the scar?

I knew that I knew *something* about the scar. Somewhere, a memory was floating around regarding it. I couldn't grasp it. A jellyfish memory.

I grabbed one of the passing crewmates.

"What is the scar?"

"The Scar! The scar! The Portal!"
Helpful.

I wandered through the deck for a while, finally taking in the surroundings. We were still several thousand feet in the air, floating through the clouds.

Above the captain's quarters were the inscribed letters:

"Condemnant quod non intellegunt"

"They condemn what they do not understand."

The crewmates were gathered around various parts of the deck. String bean, Hunchback, Cow Eye, they all have their nicknames, but I didn't know their actual names.

So I asked for them.

I turned to the line of men and stared them right in the eye.

"As the captain," I began, "I need to know all of your names."

A roar from the men. A cheer. They lifted each other high on each other's shoulders and threw each other to the deck. They reassembled into their line formation, and each saluted in turn.

String bean spoke first.

"Seven of hearts!" he said.

Hunchback spoke second.

"Net!" he said

Cow Eye spoke third.

"NYPD outfitter!" he said.

Other crewmates spoke up.

"River Television!" one said.

"Bottle can!" another said.

One by one they went down the line, spewing out nonsense.

A spot next to me implodes in on itself, puckering at the seams. Shapes and colors of the world I left behind

*were reflected in the wound, and for a
moment, I could have slipped through
the hole and fallen onto a street side.
The wound immediately beings scarring
over, a silky white skin that's just a
little bit pearled.*

"The scar, the portal, Captain..."

The scar was a portal. A portal to
what?

I felt it flitting around but couldn't
wrap my fingers around it. It's a
delicate business, remembering things;
don't try at all and it'll flit right away
from you and you won't have any idea
when it will be back, but grab at it too
hard and you'll crush its moon jelly
body and it'll end up sliming down
through the cracks of your fingers.

Day Six

Today I would make the necessary preparations. I woke up before the sun came up and creeped out past the sleeping Annex mates. I closed the rusty door slowly and quietly, so as not to wake them.

The hallway opened in a gaping yawn and swallowed me. I tumbled down its slimy and rough gullet, down the rotting stairs, and rolled into the room with the hole to Z's stairwell. My secret entrance.

I was birthed into the stairwell, and shook off all of the embryonic dust and debris, heading up the stairs slowly, carefully, purposefully.

I knocked three times on his door. Knox.

Knox.

Knox.

I was calling out my name to him on the wood. He'd know it was me (though he would surely be expecting me and only me.)

I heard Z rustling behind the door.

A spot next to me implodes in on itself, puckering at the seams. Shapes and colors of the world I left behind were reflected in the wound, and for a moment, I could have slipped through the hole and fallen onto a street side. The wound immediately beings scarring over, a silky white skin that's just a little bit pearled.

"The scar, the portal, Captain..."

What?

What portal?

Z rustled from behind the door.

Knox. Knox.

I was knocking.

No, no wait. That's wrong. He was calling to me.

Knocks.

The door opened and he looked at me for a moment. His eyes grew large, turned into huge melons, and exploded in front of me.

"Knox."

I was sure, this time, that he was calling my name.

My old friend pulled me into a tight embrace. He smelled musty. His space was not as clean as I had remembered.

I was dripping dust everywhere.

Z smelled like dust.

I turned back around and stared back down the stairs where I had recently shed a body load of dust and debris.

Z was scattered about on the steps leading up to his space.

I had to collect him up.

In a jar, maybe, or in a can, if I couldn't find a jar. He'd need a nice shelf, in my space. I would hold the can at night with me, and maybe sometimes put some of the dust on my coat before I went out to work at my store. I would deposit Z across the Normal world. I wondered if he'd like that. I wondered if he'd want to go that way.

I looked back up at Z.

He was not dust. No, no of course not.

He was right in front of me. Is right in front of me.

We had stopped hugging.

He looked at me with the melon eyes.

"Come, Knox, come inside."

He grabbed my hand and pulled me through the threshold. My fingers were putty, and stretched out way in front of me, flapping down from the grip of his fingers and dragging on the floor.

He should stop pulling so hard or they might split right off.

(*turn.*)

He sat me down on the couch I had been on just a few days before (or was it years, now?) and put a hand on my knee.

"Knox, what have you come here for? Is it what I fear?"

Fear, fear, dear, near.

"Knox, what have you come here for."

What have you come here for?

I woke up early to make the necessary preparations.

"Chains, Z, I'm here for O."

He nodded.

"I figured it would come to this, Knox. Please, follow me."

He was not afraid of me. He should be afraid of me.

He grabbed my putty fingers again, but this time was careful to fold up the lines of putty so that they wouldn't drag on the ground. How courteous, I thought, how courteous of my old and dear friend.

This time, I was lead into one of the locked rooms.

Five locks.

One two three four five.

Metal, metal, metal, metal, metal.

He had a key for each, and slipped them all in at once.

What was Z's abnormality?

I couldn't remember.

He slipped them all in at once.

Turn, click. (*turn.*)

The door swung open. Rusty, loud, it screamed in my face and ripped through my ears.

Shut up! Shut up!

The door swung to a stop, and Z pulled me in.

(Why is he pulling me, again?)

"Z," It was important, I remember, a necessity, "chains. I need them. I need to stay in this room, for a while, I think."

He smiled gently and laughed a little.

Dear Z.

"Yes, Knox, yes you do."

I do, I do, I do, skip to my lou. (*turn.*)

"Knox, please listen to me."

He grabbed my face firmly between his Normal fingers so that I could not look away.

"You cannot stay here now. Come back later, yes, that you must do (and do not forget to do it), but for now, Knox, you have to go back to your Annex mates. Do not just disappear on them. You know as well as I that they need you. Sophia, Jeffrey, even Gabriel. Do not leave them there wondering."

Sophia, Jeffrey, and Gabriel. Jeffrey. Jeffrey.

What was it that I had to remember?

Jeffrey.

A spot next to me implodes in on itself, puckering at the seams. Shapes and colors of the world I left behind were reflected in the wound, and for a moment, I could have slipped through the hole and fallen onto a street side.

"The scar, the portal, Captain..."

"Knox.."

Z was looking at me again.

"Yes, I will not stay now. Jeffrey."

He was pained.

Was it because of how I was now, or was it because of Jeffrey?

He was letting me go back for him.

My dear old friend Z.

"Z," it was important again, "the chains..."

Normal fingers walked across the barren room and grabbed a handful of metal hanging from the wall. He shook it. Shake, shake, shake.

Rattle, rattle, rattle.

"These will hold you Knox."

I walked over to the wall with the dangling lines of metal and held my hands up. My body made the shape of a T. The metal was cold.

I caught a glimpse of Z.

A tear.

Crying, he was dripping.

Sophia, but from the eyes.

(*turn.*)

"Alright."

Z came back when I spoke. His eyes dried and he motioned for me to follow him out of the room.

He re-locked all of the locks on the door.

I would be safe in there.

He would be safe out here.

A spot next to me implodes in on itself, puckering at the seams. Shapes

and colors of the world I left behind
were reflected in the wound, and for a
moment, I could have slipped through
the hole and fallen onto a street side.
The wound immediately beings scarring
over, a silky white skin that's just a
little bit pearled.

"*The scar, the portal, Captain…*"

"Go back to the Annex, Knox. Do
what you must, see who you need to
see, do not hurry back, but you *must*
remember to return."

Of course, of course.

"Yes."

Had I answered him?

I will not stay in the Annex for
long, Z, I will return here soon, Z.

I walked towards the dusty
threshold to the stairwell and continued
forward, not stopping to look back at
my dear old friend, my Z.

I heard him weeping, quietly, mutely, a mouse's cry.

What was Z's Abnormality?

(*turn.*)

I ran through the piles of dust and the piles of debris and threw myself through the hole in the wall. I tumbled out in the mill. The dank, dusty, morbid mill.

There was a crack in the impenetrable mill wall. A beam of sharp light cut through the small space, and burned into my skin.

The Normal world.

A spot next to me implodes in on itself, puckering at the seams. Shapes and colors of the world I left behind were reflected in the wound, and for a moment, I could have slipped through the hole and fallen onto a street side.

"The scar, the portal, Captain…"

The Normal world.

I slid my hand through the crack and wriggled my fingers around. They had solidified since leaving Z's space and were no longer putty.

Some of the building crumbled away when I wiggled my fingers.

So I thrashed them about wildly.

The wall rained bits of plaster and old brick.

Tink tink tink tink tink.

They all fell to the floor.

I kept digging at the wall, with an intensity I remembered, but could not fully recall. It's a delicate business, remembering things; don't try at all and it'll flit right away from you and you won't have any idea when it will be back, but grab at it too hard and you'll crush its moon jelly body and it'll end up sliming down through the cracks of your fingers.

Bigger, and bigger, and bigger, it kept growing, and stretching, and reaching. My fingers were bloody, now. Bloody stubs that were dripping over the fallen brick. The red mess on the floor made a clay of sorts and I stopped digging for a moment to grab a handful of the clay. I squished it hard between my fingers and let it drip to the ground.

A drip castle in the mill.

I turned my attention back to the wall with a new fervor. Within a few seconds (minutes, hours) the hole was big enough for me to fit through if I lifted up my left leg and angled it through, then twisted my shoulder and head to the side so that they wouldn't snag on the bloody mess of a wall.

(*turn.*)

I was through, and in the sunlight.

I realized immediately that I had fallen right into the Eye's feeding ground. They would be circling me, waiting to move in and pounce if they had the chance.

I wouldn't give them that chance.

I bolted as fast as I could out aimlessly from the mill into the city.

I ran, and ran and ran and ran.

I came to a stop in front of the Official building.

Thousands of grey boxes were walking around me, and I was stopped in the middle of the grey city. Water flowing around a rock.

They were all buzzing, moving, bustling, buzzing, Jeffrey, Jeffrey, Jeffrey.

Some of them began to notice me stopped in the middle of the sidewalk in my odd manner. I looked down at my bloody fingers and gasped.

I quickly tucked them into my coat pocket.

Blood seeped through the grey suit, and stained my pockets. I could feel it running down my legs, but the sight of the bloody nubs was revolting, and I kept them in my pockets.

Drip, drip, drip.

(*turn.*)

I looked up.

A suit was staring at me. A faceless mask that reflected only my body and bloody pockets. A blue fabric eyeball stared at me, through me, from the jackets lapel.

I did not run. I did not stand still. I walked slowly, blending with the buzzing crowd so that I would not stand out further.

I became caught up in the rip tide.

Telescreens were flashing and buzzing.

> Do not forget your copy of the
> Code Of Law when leaving your
> house in the morning.
> Please operate with regard to
> standard law.
> Thank your Officers for their
> duty; report all suspected
> Abnormals to your districts
> Office.
> Curfew tonight is set for 22:00.
> Do not forget: Taxes are due next
> quarter!

There was static, though, and I knew I had it all wrong.

> Do not forget your copy of the
> Code Of Law when leaving your
> house in the morning.

Please operate with regard to standard law.

Thank your Officers for their duty; report all suspected Abnormals to your districts Office.

Curfew tonight is set for 22:00.

Do not forget: Taxes are due next quarter!

No, no, no, it was all wrong.

The telescreens were not looping my well-memorized lines.

A black suit with a large official insignia pin on the lapel was shaking hands with another suit on the telescreen instead. A caption: Peace Negotiations Halted.

The shot was from the knees to the chest of these suits. No feet, no faces.

The Brain.

I stopped watching the telescreen long enough to hear the conversation of the grey boxes.

"Blah blah blah, blah blah Blah blah nuclear blah blah?"

"Blah blah blah, blah war blah blah Brain blah blah."

"Imminent?"

"Blah blah blah, yes."

The shaking hands of the Brain and another Official.

Nuclear.

Imminent.

Yes.

No, no, no!

A spot next to me implodes in on itself, puckering at the seams. Shapes and colors of the world I left behind were reflected in the wound, and for a moment, I could have slipped through the hole and fallen onto a street side.

"The scar, the portal, Captain…"

I was back on the street and I ran back to the mill.

I was running against the sea of buzzing boxes; panicked boxes, serious boxes, nuclear war.

I passed no Eyes, but stirred up a cloud of dust as I ran through the dry lot of the mill.

I dove back through my bloody hole, and landed in the pile of bloody mud paste. I was covered.

"You must go back for them, they need you, do not just disappear on them."

I needed to get back to the Annex.

I ran through walls of light, not caring that I was getting battered and bruised by their thick opaqueness. I swung open the rusty door to the Annex. It screamed on the hinges and I stood gasping for breath in the doorway.

Gabriel and Sophia were sitting together in the den area, and I was in the doorway directly across from them, dripping blood and paste.

A spot next to me implodes in on itself, puckering at the seams. Shapes and colors of the world I left behind were reflected in the wound, and for a moment, I could have slipped through the hole and fallen onto a street side.

"The scar, the portal, Captain..."

Jeffrey, Jeffrey, where was Jeffrey?

"Knox!"

It was a collective scream, half gasp, half shriek.

Gabriel threw an arm out in front of Sophia and was ready to lunge for me.

He thought I was going to...

No no no! No I was not!

"Gabriel! No! No! No I am not! Gabriel there is a portal! Sophia, Jeffrey! There is a portal, I've seen it! A portal! It's there! Gabriel! Sophia! Jeffrey! Oh Jeffrey, it's there!"

Everything was silent.

Gabriel was on me in an instant, and had me restrained.

"Knox, Knox, stop it! Stop moving, you can't be trusted, now."

I was enraged and desperate.

"No Gabriel, no! You don't understand! I've made the necessary preparations! You will be ok! I'm going away! I'm leaving now! *But there's a portal!* A portal to something, something, something...I don't know what it is, but *we have to find it!*"

He looked at me and my ten heads and tightened his grip.

"Leave the Annex, Knox. Get out. Leave everyone alone. You've fucked it up, Knox. Where's the money, Knox? This has done us *nothing*. Get out, now, get out before you hurt somebody."

Sophia was watching, terrified, her beautiful blue eyes wide with wonder and fear. I looked at her, locked eyes and pleaded with her silently. I would not hurt her. I would not hurt Gabriel. I would not hurt Jeffrey.

I was going away.

I turned silently and left through the Annex door. I closed it, gently, and it cried rusty tears.

There was no reason to run back to the stairwell.

I walked through the mill slowly. My last walk through the mill I had known so well.

My home.

I closed my eyes and wandered the hallways, running my raw and bloody fingers along the walls. They would see this, later, and think that I had been mad, that I had killed something and ran around in the halls. I was saying goodbye to an old friend.

My oldest friend, perhaps.

I let the moldy plaster and dust fill my cuts; I let myself become part of the mill.

I wondered how long it would take before the walls absorbed the blood. Until my blood became part of the old building.

I would remind Z to close up the hole at the bottom of the stairs.

Perhaps in a few years if things were better, and if Z fed me regularly despite the dangers, perhaps in a few years I could break back through the hole and find the Annex. Maybe I would even remember how to get around in the mill. Maybe Gabriel and Sophia and Jeffrey would still be there, too.

For now, though, I had to get to Z.

I stumbled through the threshold and fell onto Z's lap.

I cried, and he held my head and cried too, a little.

He patted my hair and after a while, stood up and led me to the five lock room.

Lock lock lock lock lock.

I walked over to the wall, to the dangling metal chains, the shackles, and held my arms up to be locked in place.

~*~

"Shapes and colors of the world I left behind were reflected in the wound, and for a moment, I could have slipped through the hole and fallen onto a street side."

The scar was a portal to the world. I became much, much more interested in the scar after this realization. I needed to find it.

Instead of taking names or watching the odd assortment of Abnormals fiddle around on the deck, I grabbed my captain's hat and put it on securely. I walked up to the wheel and grabbed it. The ship was currently spinning in circles; not tight, but large, loose swipes, the movement of a ship unmanned. I held the wheel tight, and it strained against my hands. It wanted to keep circling, not moving forward, not moving backward.

We went straight through a cloudbank. The front of the ship entered first, peeking through the thick fog. In a moment, we were completely enveloped. I could not see my hands out in front of me. I looked around. I could not see the crew, but I could hear their mutterings and could hear their steady work.

I set the wheel forward and stepped away from it. I could not steer, I could not see.

I walked through the white fog; it pushed aside to make room for my body, then quickly enveloped the empty space behind me. I walked in this fashion until I came to the side of the ship, grabbed the wheel, and followed it with my hands. I walked and walked and walked along the side of the ship, holding the rail, until I bumped into a thick object. Soft, a man. The bump jostled him but he did not stop working.

"You, good sir, how do we lower this ship?"

"Release the floaters! Release the floaters!"

The floaters.

The crew erupted in cheers of "Release the floaters!"

I was shuffled by a mass of crew hands to the floating and oversized cow eyeballs. They were still massive, and over inflated, and they were still blue, and still just as bright as when they had been removed. They tugged against the ropes that were holding them down, the ropes leaving thick and bubbled impressions in the eyes. I reached for the tough rope and wrapped my hand around it. My fingertips stuck slightly into the cow eye, and they came out covered in a thick slime. I wiped that off on the rope, and tugged at it until my hands were raw and bloody.

The bone knife.

I pulled it out from my pocket and slid it along the thick rope. It frayed immediately and was split completely in much less time than I had spent tugging with my hands. They eyeball was un-tethered and the ship took an immediate drop downward a few hundred feet.

We were out of the clouds, and
flying though clear blue air.
And then I woke up.

Day Seven

*Whatever happens, whatever I do, whatever I say, whatever I ask of you, what ever I beg of you...*physical restraints refers to the practice of rendering an animal harmless or keeping harmless or keep them in captivity chains chainainainained to the wall of rendering people dangerous of people harmless before anything happened to the people the people the Jeffrey Gabriel Sophia Z if this is just another stage if this is just another if its just promise me the restraints, ties, fastens, secures, chains, ropes, bolts

and locks, five locks onetwothreefourfive
metal secures control and caution and
caution and reserve and a limb restraint
is the wall of a filthy room for two
months a better room better than mill
space wall in the room with five locks
and the dirt and the dust and the dirt
and the mud and grass and fencenence
and the blood the blood and the gun and
the glass sidewalk smoothmothersdress
is all bloody now, mother is all bloody
now, mother is all, Sophia, the buzzing
the buzzing a refrigerator, detuned
radio static andandand tethered by their
necks in heavy iron chains to the wall
become dangerous keep me on
oxydangerous fed only bread harm to
himself or others solid week of work
fastening, ties, limb restraint but please
promise me that you'll keep me cuffs
and shackles the act of controlling do

not let him stop me Gabriel stop me
taking if I become dangerous keep me
on the oxymorptivity trying to prevent
Jeffrey from happening again, if
anything is going to happen chain me
up with arms and legs and necks the
men sobbed whatever happens
whatever say I get a job we know I
have a solid week of work, if anything
is go to the cold, the metal, the
hardcoldchainsbolts, I have to know, by
now you must chain me up the medical
restraints are applied to the arms and
legs of a patient and were repeatedly
beaten during theireireir captivity, the
men sobbed uncontrollably when they
saw their rescucucucuers by their necks
with heavyironbeaten sticks handcuffs
and shackles days during their captivity
shackled to the O I need to know must
need know if Jeffrey will happen again

when they come dangerous even you
must promise—stop, look, stop, I'm not
sayayayaying that's going to happen I
saw their rescuers the chains to the wall
just another stage with bread and water
every few days prevent the patient
water every few days during their
captivity with metal locks shackled for
a solid week before they saw their
rescuers—

~*~

The ship was now only a hundred feet above the water. We were under the clouds, and able to see for miles ahead. We were in no city. We were, currently, flying over the countryside; green rolling hills, purple tipped mountains, and clear blue water. It looked cold, and there were large fish swimming around in the shadow of our ship.

String Bean was standing near me, gazing out over the water and over the mountains. The crew had taken on a new mood; the incessant chattering had stopped, and foolish nonsense had pretty much dissipated— they were now all gathered together, staring out in the direction we were traveling, all searching, all hoping, for what I could only assume was this portal. The scar. The point where it all started, and the point where it all puckered back in on itself and ended.

He looked over at me, their captain, and watched the wheel move back and forth between my arms.

"Mr. Ian Woon was our first captain."

What? He was talking to me.

"Aye, yes sir Captain, he was. He found the portal, you know. Well, not found— he discovered it. Well, that's not even quite right. He discovered its purpose is. What it does. Aye, yes sir. Captain."

He was nervous, and turned back to look outward.

There was a silence. I held the creaking wheel tight, and he continued staring outward over the ocean to some invisible attraction.

"That so?"

He turned back to me, still nervous, but now slightly more assured.

"Aye. Yes sir, Captain. Figured it out, he did."

Hmm. That so.

"What… what is it, exactly. What is the portal going *to*?"

He slipped back into his nervous tone, but turned to face me. He took a few steps closer, and lowered his voice.

"That's the thing. We don't really know. We think we know, but of course there is no way for us to be positive."

He fidgeted around some with his hands and looked back up at me, timidly, a child telling a secret.

"To the Normal world."

The Normal world. I wake up and I'm in the Normal world. I felt cheated.

"But it is entirely different."

"How so, how is it different?"

I was intrigued.

"We can be there. As Abnormals, I mean. We can be there, outside and around other people, and no one says a thing. No one screams, no one beats us, no one shuffles us away in a van, no one shoots at us, we just… live. As Abnormals. With the abnormalities. We can live freely, you know, we can live without running on this ship all the time. Been on here for years, you know. Sick of it. Sick of all of it."

I sympathized. I'd been in the mill for years.

But a world, a normal world, where we could live out with the rest of the people? No, no, it was a mistake. He was mistaken. A world like that didn't exist. Couldn't.

I couldn't fathom it. Couldn't wrap my head around it.

Could it?

He had turned back seaward and was looking out over the mountains. For the portal, for the scar, for a chance to live freely.

I slumped over the wheel slightly, baffled completely by his words.

Sophia could be a Normal woman, if she wanted to, and could even maybe eventually fix the harelip. They had surgeries for that, I believe, not that an Abnormal could ever afford one or could ever escape into the sunlight for long enough to find a clinic. But she could if she could go out safely...

And Gabriel! He would be much more pleasant, I think, if he could be in charge of his life, for once. If he wasn't trapped like an animal at all times. He could be completely Normal. Besides, he was practically Normal now, except for the tourettes...

And Jeffrey. My beautiful Jeffrey, fair-haired, delicate face— could he even be alone in the Normal world? No, no of course not, he would need someone, would need me (at least I liked to think so, I would sure as hell need him), he couldn't live entirely alone. He'd need someone to bring him back. To introduce him to everything. Hell, all of the Annex-mates would need someone to introduce them to the

Normal world. And who better suited than me? I had been out for a week, after all, in the Normal world, doing trivial tasks.

I wanted to find the portal now more than ever.

"Hey."

He turned back around and faced me, his face lit up.

"Tell me more about the captains."

He turned his body around and came closer. He took a deep breath, and began:

"After Mr. Ian Woon, Naomi Worn was captain. First girl captain. Only girl captain. She was a vixen and a tornado. A powerhouse. Small, thin, very pretty, with fiery red hair and a fiery red personality. Bad temper, too. But attractive. Ask any of the crewmates. She was good at what she did, though.

Very good. Heard of Mr. Ian Woon's legacy and was determined to find the portal. They all were. But her especially. She was deformed in the face. Had a big scar looking birthmark from her right temple down to her chin. Still a stunner, but boy was she bitter about that birthmark. Hated it, hated it, hated it."

He paused for another breath.

"She took us pretty far. Got us just about there. Then one day, she was feeling up that mark for a while, then she'd stop and get back to directing us, but her hand would keep finding that spot, and her little fingers would trace it over and over and over, trying to make it go away, or reminding herself that it was there. Maybe she was using it as an inspiration to get to the portal. I don't know. But anyway, she was feeling that scar for a while, and when she took a break to go to the captain's quarters for lunch, she didn't come back out. A few of us went in to get her, see what she wanted us to do, and there she was, slumped over that table in there, lying a puddle of her own blood."

Breath.

"Everywhere, it was. She had ripped that birthmark right off, and had bled to death because of it. A whole chunk of her face was gone from the temple down, and her nails and fingers were all bloody and dripping. Well, we were upset, and naturally there was a bit of chaos without our captain, so we cleaned her up some and cleaned up the quarters all nice (you can't even see the blood anymore, or you would have noticed it before) and we cleaned her up all nice too, and a few of the guys took her for a while, but most just hung around on the deck. When they brought her back out, we chopped her up and fed her to the cows. Not much else to do with a dead body on this boat. Straight to the cows!"

Red hair poking out of the muscled cow's exposed teeth. I was repulsed by the image.

"What happened then? What did you do without a captain?"

"Nothing. We just sat around in the sky for a while, not knowing what to do. There was talk of electing a new captain, but none of us knew how to do that, no sir. So we sat around just floating for a long, long time. Eventually, the talk of electing a new captain became more serious, because we weren't getting anywhere fast at that pace, and we all still wanted to find that portal, so we held an election in the captain's quarters. Hunchback got the most votes, but before they were tallied, a new guy showed up. Fry, we called him. He was calm, and determined to help, to find the portal. He was just what we needed after Naomi. Water to the fire. He was our rock, and we quickly elected him captain instead. Things with him were great; better than with any other captain."

He looked at me uncomfortably, suddenly, seeing if he had offended me.

He hadn't.

"He was perfect at his job, no slacking, no breaks, the poor guy didn't even stop to eat he was so determined to find the portal. It meant a lot to him, it did, and we all thought that he'd be our last captain, that he'd finally find it."

"And what happened? Obviously you didn't find the portal... what happened with Fry?"

He smiled his bashful smile again, and continued.

"He just disappeared one day. Went into the captains quarters, and didn't come out. Now we were fearing the worst. We thought for sure that we were gonna find him face down in a puddle of blood, after Naomi and all, so we went in with rags and water for cleaning purposes. But he wasn't in there. Wasn't anywhere on the whole ship. We looked and looked and looked for days. He was just gone.

That was a pretty bad loss for us, you know? He meant a lot to the crew. Kept us all sane. Kept us all motivated. His passion for the portal affected us a lot, we couldn't avoid it. It was like the enthusiasm of a little kid; you might sometimes stop thinking something's possible, might stop believing that there is such a thing as a portal to a safe normal world for a while, but when you hear that little kid talking about it like it's the surest thing in the world and the greatest thing in the world, you can't help but hope that it's really real, if just for that kid. You don't ever let on that you don't think it's real, just in case you hurt the poor guy's spirit, and playing it up like you believe it eventually makes you come around and start believing it yourself. Self-deception. I was afraid that after we lost him, the crew would lose hope again. So we got to the elections faster this time, to keep the momentum up, and we picked Hunchback, since he had been our original contender, and he put on the hat and played the role alright.

Until you showed up, that is."

He looked to the hat on my head and continued.

"A natural captain, you are. A lot like Fry, but real different too. And that's where we're at now."

There were a few moments of quiet between us, wind whipping the fleshy sails around in a flapping melody.

"So are you telling me that sometimes you didn't believe in the portal?"

He was hesitant for a moment, then turned to look at me full on.

"Yes, Captain, thought it was a load of malarkey."

"So how do we know it's real? How do we know it's real if you only still

look for it because you made yourself
for the sake of this guy's feelings?"

He was gravely serious.

"Well, you saw it, didn't you
Captain? You saw it, the scar when you
first got here, you saw it right?"

I had.

"We're getting closer. We need to
drop another floater."

He said it more to the wind than to
me. He was already walking back to the
rail to look out over the mountains. I
turned to the rest of the crew to do my
job as Captain.

"Drop a floater! Get us lower"

Four crewmates ran over to the
tethered eyeballs and tore the rope
away near one. It floated upward fast,
and the boat dropped at an alarming
rate. We neared the speed of light, and
we were fast approaching the water.

We were going to crash, and the boat was going to splinter into a million pieces, but it stopped mere inches above the raging waves. Salt water spit up at us as we skimmed over the water at the pace of a speedboat. The deck would be covered with salty brine within the day.

I focused back on the wheel, and kept us steady forward towards String Bean's line of sight.

I got to thinking about the portal, about the ship of Abnormals, and about the captains.

I was here only because of O induced dreaming. I knew that much. So what did that mean for the truth of the portal? Was it real; was I in a different world, a different plane of existence only accessible in my sleep? I hoped so. I needed this portal to be real, now more than ever.

But if that were true, would that mean that all of the other Abnormals on here were all in their own O induced dreams? Was this a mutual meeting ground for the drugged? Did everyone on O have this same dream? Did Jeffrey ever meet up with these people on this ship?

Then there was always the possibility that is was all in my head--a dream and a land exclusive to me. But if that was the case, would the dream lead me to a portal meant for me to find? Would it reveal a location in my waking world so that I could access it? So many questions, so many unanswerable, burning questions…

There was an electricity in the mood on the ship. Everyone was working towards the same goal, regardless of whether or not they were just figments of my over-drugged mind or real people. At that moment, the lunacy of the ship had dulled to near non-existent, and we were all united by the hope and yearning for an alternate Normal world.

We were close to the portal. I could feel it. Tugging, tugging, harder as we moved closer.

The ship needed to hit water.

"Drop the last floater! Get this ship on the water!"

I was a complete authority figure; the crew united and un-tethered the last eyeball. The over-inflated blue cow eye drifted away into the sky, disappearing behind the clouds; the last trace of the nonsensical ship I had arrived on during my first day. The boat was now completely normal, grounded in reality, save for the Abnormals running its decks. Dream had become reality, or a close second for reality.

We hit the water hard. The smoothness of motion was replaced by the choppiness of roiling waves; we held our ground well, considering.

String Bean turned and looked me in the eye. We were fast approaching our destination, we both felt it.

Then a thought...

"Hey, that captain, Fry, the one that disappeared... was his real name—"

The boat crashed hard into the rocky shore, throwing the crew around on the decks and causing us to lose our footing. It kept going, though, propelled forward by sheer momentum. The bottom of the ship was grinding away to nothing; wood splinters were flying around us and large chunks were being ripped from the boat.

We were still moving a hundred miles an hour.

Trees and hills blurred by us, and we sank lower and lower to the ground as the ship was ripped away to nothing. We were speeding forward, and there was a shape in the distance. I started moving forward, but was stopped. I was stuck, and I yanked forward, hard against my invisible captor. The shape grew larger and larger and the air around us was positively electric. I ripped free from my binding and ran towards the front of the ship to get a clear view of the object now directly in front of us.

A wall. A single standing wall, with large chunks of the plaster removed. Holes in the wall big enough for a person. Many, many holes, all empty, then finally one filled—a rip in the fabric of the world leading directly to the street corner...

Shapes and colors of the world I left behind were reflected in the wound, and for a moment, I could have slipped through the hole and fallen onto a street side.

The portal.

Sophia's Story

At this point, it is necessary that I take over. Unfortunately, Knox does not remember the following moments, and was in fact not present for some of them. The bits he was present for--well, the O had taken full control of him by that point, and one cannot blame him for not remembering. (Sometimes we wonder if he was even truly present for them.) Knox's story and information would clear up some ambiguities that inevitably remain for me, Gabriel, and Jeffrey, but again, given his state, one cannot blame him.

It was not until several days after Knox broke through the door covered in blood and mud that anything significant happened. Of course, you may count our conversation and actions once he left the Annex significant, so I will indulge you.

We woke up that morning to find Knox already missing. I remember being immediately worried about him; I remembered our conversation when he first started treatment, and hoped that he hadn't snapped and gotten himself captured by the Eyes or Ears.

You just don't know, with Knox. Especially when he is affected in such a way.

While I was sick with worry, Gabriel was quiet. He must have been worried too, although he was also probably relieved that he wouldn't have to worry about being attacked again by an over-drugged O.

And Jeffrey was, as always, in the kitchen.

He seemed to notice that Knox was gone, too. He always seems to clear up slightly around Knox, especially since he began the O treatment. I'll admit that it was a little frustrating that Gabriel and myself could not get him to look at us or respond the way Knox could.

That morning, the morning that Knox went missing, Jeffrey had stopped digging his holes. Completely stopped. It was eerie, and I think even Gabriel was a little worried at this point. Jeffrey would just sit in the corner of the kitchen, holding that rotting apple that Knox had given him. He just sat like that all day--until Knox showed up later.

Gabriel and I were sitting in the living area, discussing the situation. He was convinced that Knox had snapped, and that he was not safe. He wanted to find the remaining funds from Knox's week of work and spend it on some metal bars so that we could close off the Annex entirely, in case Knox tried to come back. I thought that was a terrible, terrible thing to do, to spend the money he made to keep him out, but Gabriel's logic was strong, and I couldn't argue with him.

Right around that time, Jeffrey began calling out. It startled Gabriel and I, to be sure. He had not spoken (to us, at least) for longer than we could remember. But we heard him calling out from the kitchen. It was a weak murmur at first that turned into a full-blown wail. He was calling for Knox.

He just sat there on the floor, yelling his name, over and over.

It was a premonition, of sorts, I guess. We didn't know that at the time though.

Shortly after Jeffrey began calling out to him, Knox comes in and busts down the door directly across from us, dripping what looked like blood and some sort of tacky paste.

"Knox!" Jeffrey was still calling to him, even after he broke through the door.

I screamed out of sheer shock. We were not expecting that, at all. Gabriel screamed too, out of shock at first, but then out of fear.

Gabriel ended up covering me with his arms to protect me from the thing standing in the doorway. He thought that Knox was going to attack us—

there are rare moments when Gabriel is completely selfless; this was one of them.

Then Knox started spewing out a bunch of garble about a portal.

"Gabriel! No! No! No I am not! Gabriel there is a portal! Sophia, Jeffrey! There is a portal, I've seen it! A portal! It's there! Gabriel! Sophia! Jeffrey! Oh Jeffrey, it's there!"

Everything was silent for a while after this. We thought that he was crazy. Even Jeffrey had stopped calling his name (though we would later realize that he had resumed digging after Knox's odd speech.)

Gabriel jumped up from the floor and was on Knox, holding him against the wall so that he could not move.

"Knox, Knox, stop it! Stop moving, you can't be trusted, now."

Knox still looked wild, bewildered. He wasn't fighting Gabriel's restraints, either. I think it was now that I realized that things were different than we had first thought.

"No Gabriel, no! You don't understand! I've made the necessary preparations! You will be ok! I'm going away! I'm leaving now! *But there's a portal!* A portal to something, something, something...I don't know what it is, but *we have to find it!*"

Again with the talk of a portal--he sounded so desperate.

Gabriel couldn't see what I saw in his odd behavior, though, and only tightened his grip on Knox.

"Leave the Annex, Knox. Get out. Leave everyone alone. You've fucked it up, Knox. Where's the money, Knox?

This has done us *nothing*. Get out, now, get out before you hurt somebody."

Knox looked at me, then. He had given up, I could see it. But I could see something else, too. He was still rational. I could see a spark of the old Knox in his eyes. He looked at me the way he had when he first convinced me that O was a good idea. By then, I was completely sure that he was not going to hurt any of us.

He turned around, then, and left. I cried as he closed the door.

After that incident, Gabriel was even more convinced that we had to close off the Annex somehow. I tried to convince him that Knox would not hurt us, but he was not having any of that. He dug around in the Annex for quite some time during the next few days, looking for Knox's money. While he didn't find money for the longest time, he did find the large chocolate wrappers that Knox had taken home. He also found a receipt for a bottle of syrup, and was furious.

(To be honest, I was a little upset too. Not so much that he had spent the money on candies and other indulgences, but because he did not tell me about them. He probably had his reasons, I realized, but I felt slightly betrayed.)

By the end of those few days, he had only found thirty cents.

For a while after that, Gabriel and I sat together trying to find a solution to our troubles. Thirty cents would only buy a bit of scrap metal, and Gabriel feared that it would not be enough to keep Knox out. We threw around many, many ideas. A temporary Oxymorphin fix was even considered, so that Gabriel could keep his tourettes under control for long enough to make a day's salary in the Normal world. Knox had the O, though, and Gabriel was vehemently opposed to the idea.

In the end, we decided that we would settle for the scrap metal that the thirty cents would buy us.

The next morning, Gabriel woke up early enough to leave the Annex before the sun was up. He planned to see if he could find Cynthia to buy metal off of her. We did not know if she was still making rounds to the mill since we had all cut off contact with her, but it was our only real hope.

I watched him leave that morning, and stayed by the entrance to the mill.

I waited.

And waited.

And before long, it was bright outside, and Gabriel was not back.

Worried, I walked out to the hidden entrance and looked out for him.

He was running desperately across the mill lot. No metal, nothing.

He caught me in the doorway and grabbed me quickly so as to move me away from the door. He got inside and slammed it, grabbing anything and everything he could to block the door. I was terrified; I had no idea what was going on. He yelled at me to go back upstairs, to secure the Annex, to hide, to run away, he yelled things that weren't even words, just animal noises and screams.

So I ran.

I ran through the hallways of the mill, cutting my arm on jutting pipes and falling over broken boards and lumps of debris. I saw streaks of blood on the walls and was suddenly terrified that Knox had escaped, somehow, and that he had killed someone already.

I made it back to the Annex as quickly as possible.

I hid as much as I could, and left the door open for Gabriel; he would not have wanted that, but I was not going to leave him out there, trapped in the hallway with whatever it was that he was running from.

I hid, myself, and tried to hide Jeffrey. He would not move though, and was intent on digging away at the walls. In my panic, I didn't even care. *Fuck Jeffrey*, I remember thinking. He was going to get himself killed.

Right then, Gabriel burst through the doorway, gasping and panting wildly, and threw himself in a corner, ready to hide or fight.

"Gabriel, what—"

"--the eyes! Officials! Followed—mill..."

Before he could finish, there was a loud explosion from downstairs, and all the noises of the city were now flooding all of the hallways and corners in the mill.

There were screams of panic and riot, ringing metal and explosions from the streets, and one reverberating voice echoing as if from every building and street corner saying (as if on a loop), "I'm sorry, I'm sorry, I'm sorry, I'm sorry, I'm sorry..."

The next moments were a blur.

There was a deafening crash and roar of falling brick and plaster, and the footsteps of a hundred Officials were

heard running through the hallways—
doors were being ripped down, tenants
were being captured and killed—

There was an ear splitting screech
of tearing metal, and a blood-curdling
scream from right outside our door.

Then it was ripped to the ground.

There Knox stood, snarling wildly,
foaming, vomiting, and oozing black
froth, his eyes glazed over entirely, a
sleep walking monstrosity— chains and
shackles hung from his bloody arms,
and he lunged forward towards us...

For a moment, time stopped. One
last crumb of plaster fell from the wall
in the kitchen, and we were engulfed in
a white light—

Knox (Again —)

I woke up to a blinding white light.
The white light from the dreams. The
puckering scar from the dreams.

*Shapes and colors of the world I left
behind were reflected in the wound,
and for a moment, I could have slipped
through the hole and fallen onto a
street side.*

We all grabbed hands and—
"Jeffrey! You've—!"

FIN